FAMOUS IRISH
GHOST STORIES

FAMOUS IRISH
GHOST STORIES

Edited by Mairtin O'Griofa
Illustrated by Sheila Kern

A Sterling/Main Street Book
Sterling Publishing Co., Inc.   New York

Library of Congress Cataloging-in-Publication Data

Famous Irish ghost stories / edited by Mairtin O'Griofa ; illustrated
by Sheila Kern.
       p.   cm.
   Includes index.
   ISBN 0-8069-0708-8
   1. Ghost stories, English—Irish authors.   2. Ireland—Fiction.
  I. O'Griofa, Mairtin.
  PR8876.5.G45F36   1994
  823'.08733089415—dc20   93–44263
                                           CIP

Designed by John Murphy
Typeset by Upper Case Limited, Cork, Ireland

10 9 8 7 6 5 4 3 2 1

A Sterling/Main Street Book

Published in 1994 by Sterling Publishing Company, Inc.
387 Park Avenue South, New York, N.Y. 10016
© 1994 by Sterling Publishing Company, Inc.
Distributed in Canada by Sterling Publishing
℅ Canadian Manda Group, P.O. Box 920, Station U
Toronto, Ontario, Canada M8Z 5P9
Distributed in Great Britain and Europe by Cassell PLC
Villiers House, 41/47 Strand, London WC2N 5JE, England
Distributed in Australia by Capricorn Link (Australia) Pty Ltd.
P.O. Box 6651, Baulkham Hills, Business Centre, NSW 2153,
Australia
Manufactured in the United States of America

ISBN 0-8069-0708-8

Contents

Introduction

No READER needs to be told that the supernatural plays a vital part in both the folklore and the fiction of, and about, Ireland. *Famous Irish Ghost Stories* brings together some of the best examples—most famous, some little known—of the Irish tale of terror. While short in content, the collection is long in its ability to chill one's blood and haunt one's dreams. Included among the authors are:

Patrick Kennedy (1801-1873), whose lifelong interest in Irish folk tales led to publication of his monumental *Legendary Fictions of the Irish Celts* (1866), is responsible for recording what is probably the only story about football-playing ghosts. American readers of "The Ghosts and the Game of Football" should be reminded that Irish football is more akin to soccer than to the American game of the same name.

Gerald Griffin (1803-1840), whose *Holland-Tide; or Munster Popular Tales* (1827) rivalled in popularity the romantic outpourings of his contempory Sir Walter Scott, but is now lamentably little read, greatly influenced most subsequent nineteenth-century writers of the supernatural. "The Brown Man" is typical of the macabre stories included in *Holland-Tide* and still shocks a century and a half after its first publication.

While Joseph Sheridan Le Fanu (1814-1873) is known today primarily for his pioneering tales of ratiocination, "the Irish Poe" remains paramount as one of the finest masters of supernatural fiction. "The Specter Lovers," one of his most enduring short stories, first appeared in 1851 in *Dublin University Magazine*, of which he was editor.

Jeremiah Curtin (1838-1906), an Irish-American linguist and comparative mythologist famous for his many collections of American Indian myths, also published *Tales of the Fairies and of the World of Ghosts* (1892), recorded in southwest Munster, and from which his ghoulish story of "The Blood-Drawing Ghost" is taken.

Bram Stoker (1847-1912), the Dublin-born creator of Transylvania's Count Dracula, contributed his most unChristmaslike "The Judge's House" to the Christmas issue of *Holly Leaves* magazine (1891). Over a century later, the story still raises goose bumps with alacrity.

American-born Francis Marion Crawford (1854-1901) is largely unknown to contemporary readers, although his Irish tale of the banshee, "The Dead Smile," remains a classic of the supernatural.

Oscar Wilde's (1854-1900) "The Canterville Ghost" is the perfect antidote to the heart-palpitations of the foregoing stories. Among other things, it is a brilliant satire on American manners and on the conventions of the ghost story Wilde would have grown up on in his native Ireland. It is also the most charming and sweet-tempered ghost story ever written.

Daniel Crowley and the Ghosts
Traditional

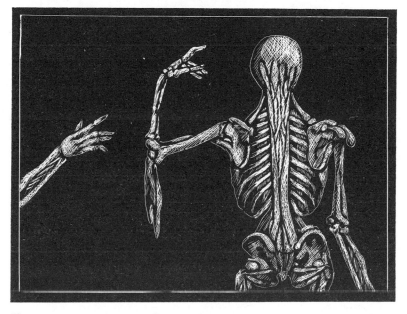

THERE LIVED A MAN IN CORK whose name was Daniel Crowley. He was a coffin-maker by trade, and had a deal of coffins laid by, so that his apprentice might sell them when himself was not at home.

A messenger came to Daniel Crowley's shop one day and told him that there was a man dead at the end of the town, and to send up a coffin for him, or to make one.

Daniel Crowley took down a coffin, put it on a donkey cart, drove to the wake house, went in and told the people of the house that the coffin was there for them. The corpse was laid out on a table in a room next to the kitchen. Five or six women were keeping watch around it; many people were in the kitchen.

Daniel Crowley was asked to sit down and commence to shorten the night: that is, to tell stories, amuse himself and others. A tumbler of punch was brought, and he promised to do the best he could.

He began to tell stories and shorten the night. A second glass of punch was brought to him, and he went on telling tales. There was a man at the wake who sang a song: after him another was found, and then another. Then the people asked Daniel Crowley to sing, and he did. The song that he sang was of another nation. He sang about the good people, the fairies. The song pleased the company, they desired him to sing again, and he did not refuse.

Daniel Crowley pleased the company so much with his two songs that a woman who had three daughters wanted to make a match for one of them and get Daniel Crowley as a husband for her. Crowley was a bachelor, well on in years, and had never thought of marrying.

The mother spoke of the match to a woman sitting next to her. The woman shook her head, but the mother said:

"If he takes one of my daughters I'll be glad, for he has money laid by. Do you go and speak to him, but say nothing of me at first.'

The woman went to Daniel Crowley then, and told him that she had a fine, beautiful girl in view, and that now was his time to get a good wife; he'd never have such a chance again.

Crowley rose up in great anger. "There isn't a woman wearing clothes that I'd marry," said he. " There isn't a woman born that could bring me to make two halves of my loaf for her."

The mother was insulted now and forget herself. She began to abuse Crowley.

"Bad luck to you, you hairy little scoundrel," said she, "you might be a grandfather to my child. You are not fit to clean the shoes on her feet. You have only dead people for company day and night; 'tis by them you make your living."

"Oh, then," said Daniel Crowley, "I'd prefer the dead to the living any day if all the living were like you. Besides, I have nothing against the dead. I am getting employment by them and not by the living, for 'tis the dead that want coffins."

"Bad luck to you, 'tis with the dead you ought to be and not with the living; 'twould be fitter for you to go out of this altogether and go to your dead people."

"I'd go if I knew how to go to them," said Crowley.

"Why not invite them to supper?" retorted the woman.

He rose up then, went out, and called:

"Men, women, children, soldiers, sailors, all people that I have ever made coffins for, I invite you tonight to my house, and I'll spend what is needed in giving a feast."

The people who were watching the dead man on the table saw him smile when he heard the invitation. They ran out of the room in a fright and out of the kitchen, and Daniel Crowley hurried away to his shop as fast as ever his donkey could carry him. On the way he came to a public-house and, going in, bought a pint bottle of whiskey, put it in his pocket, and drove on.

The workshop was locked and the shutters down when he left that evening, but when he came near he saw that all the windows were shining with light, and he was in dread that the building was burning or that robbers were in it. When right there Crowley slipped into a corner of the building opposite, to know could he see what was happening, and soon he saw crowds of men, women, and children walking toward his shop and going in, but none coming out. He was hiding some time when a man tapped him on the shoulder and asked, "Is it here you are, and we waiting for you? 'Tis a shame to treat company this way. Come now."

Crowley went with the man to the shop, and as he passed the threshold he saw a great gathering of people. Some were neighbors, people he had known in the past. All were dancing, singing, amusing themselves. He was not long looking on when a man came up to him and said:

"You seem not to know me, Daniel Crowley."

"I don't know you," said Crowley. " How could I?"

"You might then, and you ought to know me, for I am the first man you made a coffin for, and 'twas I gave you the first start in business."

Soon another came up, a lame man: "Do you know me, Daniel Crowley?"

"I do not."

"I am your cousin, and it isn't long since I died."

"Oh, now I know you well, for you are lame. In God's name," said Crowley to the cousin, "how am I to get these people out o' this. What time is it?"

"'Tis early yet, it's hardly eleven o'clock, man."

Crowley wondered that it was so early.

"Receive them kindly," said the cousin; "be good to them, make merriment as you can."

"I have no money with me to get food or drink for them; 'tis night now, and all places are closed," answered Crowley.

"Well, do the best you can," said the cousin.

The fun and dancing went on, and while Daniel Crowley was looking around, examining everything, he saw a woman in the far-off comer. She took no part in the amusement, but seemed very shy in herself.

"Why is that woman so shy—she seems to be afraid?" asked he of the cousin. "And why doesn't she dance and make merry like others?"

"Oh, 'tis not long since she died, and you gave the coffin, as she had no means of paying for it. She is in dread you'll ask her for the money, or let the company know that she didn't pay," said the cousin.

The best dancer they had was a piper by the name of John Reardon from the city of Cork. The fiddler was one John Healy. Healy brought no fiddle with him, but he made one, and the way he made it was to take off what flesh he had on his body. He rubbed up and down on his own ribs, each rib having a different note, and he made the loveliest music that Daniel Crowley had ever heard. After that the whole company followed his example. All threw off what flesh they had on them and began to dance jigs and hornpipes in their bare bones. When by chance they struck against one another in dancing, you'd think it was Brandon Mountain that was sinking Mount Eagle, with the noise that was in it.

Daniel Crowley plucked up all his courage to know could he live through the night, but still he thought daylight would never come. There was one man, John Sullivan, that he noticed especially. This man had married twice in his life, and with him came the two women. Crowley saw him taking out the second wife to dance a breakdown, and the two danced so well that the company were delighted, and all the skeletons had their mouths open, laughing. He danced and knocked so much merriment out of them all that his first wife, who was at the end of the house, became jealous and very mad altogether. She ran down to where he was and told him she had a better right to dance with him than the second wife; "That's not the truth for you," said the second wife, "I have a better right than you. When he married me you were a dead woman and he was free, and, besides, I'm a better dancer than what you are, and I will dance with him whether you like it or not."

"Hold your tongue!" screamed the first wife. "Sure, you

couldn't come to this feast tonight at all but for the loan of another woman's shinbones."

Sullivan looked at his two wives and asked the second one:

"Isn't it your own shinbones you have?"

"No, they are borrowed. I borrowed a neighboring woman's shins from her, and 'tis those I have with me tonight."

"Who is the owner of the shinbones you have under you?" asked the husband.

"They belong to one Catherine Murray. She hadn't a very good name in life."

"But why didn't you come on your own feet?"

"Oh, I wasn't good myself in life, and I was put under a penalty, and the penalty is that whenever there is a feast or a ball I cannot go to it unless I am able to borrow a pair of shins."

Sullivan was raging when he found that the shinbones he had been dancing with belonged to a third woman, and she not the best, and he gave a slap to the wife that sent her spinning into a corner.

The woman had relations among the skeletons present, and they were angry when they saw the man strike their friend. "We'll never let that go with him," said they. "We must knock satisfaction out of Sullivan!"

The woman's friends rose up, and, as there were no clubs or weapons, they pulled off their left arms and began to slash and strike with them in terrible fashion. There was an awful battle in one minute.

While this was going on Daniel Crowley was standing below at the end of the room, cold and hungry, not knowing but he'd be killed. As Sullivan was trying to dodge the blows sent against him, he got as far as Daniel Crowley and stepped on his toe without knowing it; Crowley got vexed and gave Sullivan a blow with his fist that drove the head from him and sent it flying to the opposite corner.

When Sullivan saw his head flying off from the blow, he ran, and, catching it, aimed a blow at Daniel Crowley with the head, and aimed so truly that he knocked him under the bench; then, having him at a disadvantage, Sullivan hurried to the bench and began to strangle him. He squeezed his throat and held him so firmly between the bench and the floor that the man lost his senses and couldn't remember a thing more.

When Daniel Crowley came to himself in the morning, his apprentice found him stretched under the bench with an empty bottle under his arm. He was bruised and pounded. His throat was sore where Sullivan had squeezed it; he didn't know how the company broke up, nor when his guests went away.

John Reardon and the Sister Ghosts
Traditional

ONCE THERE WAS A FARMER, a widower, Tom Reardon, who
lived near Castlemain. He had an only son, a fine strong boy,
who was almost a man, and the boy's name was John. This
farmer married a second time, and the stepmother hated the boy
and gave him neither rest nor peace. She was turning the
father's mind against the son, till at last the farmer resolved to
put the son in a place where a ghost was, and this ghost never
let any man go without killing him.

One day the father sent the son to the forge with some chains
belonging to a plow; he would have two horses plowing next
day.

The boy took the chains to the forge; and it was nearly

evening when the father sent him, and the forge was four miles away.

The smith had much work and he hadn't the chains mended till close on to midnight. The smith had two sons, and they didn't wish to let John go, but he said he must go, for he had promised to be home and the father would kill him if he stayed away. They stood before him in the door, but he went in spite of them.

When two miles from the forge a ghost rose up before John, a woman; she attacked him and they fought for two hours, when he put the plow chain round her. She could do nothing then, because what belongs to a plow is blessed. He fastened the chain and dragged the ghost home with him, and told her to go to the bedroom and give the father and stepmother a rough handling, not to spare them.

The ghost beat them till the father cried for mercy, and said if he lived till morning he'd leave the place, and that the wife was the cause of putting John in the way to be killed.

John put food on the table and told the ghost to sit down and eat for herself, but she refused and said he must take her back to the very spot where he found her. John was willing to do that, and he went with her. She told him to come to that place on the following night, that there was a sister of hers, a ghost, a deal more determined and stronger than what herself was.

John told her that maybe the two of them would attack and kill him. She said that they would not, that she wanted his help against the sister, and that he would not be sorry for helping her. He told her he would come, and when he was leaving her she said not to forget the plow chains.

Next morning the father was going to leave the house, but the wife persuaded him to stay. "That ghost will never walk the way again," said she. John went the following night, and the ghost was waiting before him on the spot where he fought with her. They walked on together two miles by a different road, and halted. They were talking in that place a while when the sister came and attacked John Reardon, and they were fighting two hours and she was getting the better of the boy, when the first sister put the plow chains around her. He pulled her home with the chains, and the first sister walked along behind them. When John came to the house, he opened the door, and when the father saw the two ghosts he said that if morning overtook him alive he'd leave the son everything, the farm and the house.

The son told the second ghost to go down and give a good turn to the stepmother; "Let her have a few strong knocks," said he.

The second ghost barely left life in the stepmother. John had food on the table, but they would not take a bite, and the second sister said he must take her back to the very spot where he met her first. He said he would. She told him that he was the bravest man that ever stood before her, and that she would not threaten him again in the world, and told him to come the next night. He said he would not, for the two might attack and get the better of him. They promised they would not attack, but would help him, for it was to get the upper hand of the youngest and strongest of the sisters that they wanted him, and that he must bring the plow chains, for without them they could do nothing.

He agreed to go if they would give their word not to harm him. They said they would give their word and would help him the best they could.

The next day, when the father was going to leave the place, the wife would not let him. "Stay where you are," she said, "they'll never trouble us again."

John went the third night, and, when he came, the two sisters were before him, and they walked till they travelled four miles then told him to stop on the green grass at one side and not to be on the road.

They weren't waiting long when the third sister came, and red lightning flashing from her mouth. She went at John, and with the first blow that she gave him put him on his knees. He rose with the help of the two sisters, and for three hours they fought, and the youngest sister was getting the better of the boy when the two others threw the chains around her. The boy dragged her away home with him then, and, when the stepmother saw the three sisters coming, herself and John's father were terrified and they died of fright, the two of them

John put food on the table and told the sisters to come and eat, but they refused, and the youngest told him that he must take her to the spot where he fought with her. All four went to that place, and at parting they promised never to harm him and to put him in the way that he would never need to do a day's work, nor his children after him, if he had any. The eldest sister told him to come on the following night, and to bring a spade with him; she would tell him, she said, her whole history from first to last.

He went, and what she told him was this: Long ago her father was one of the richest men in all Ireland; her mother died when the three sisters were very young, and ten or twelve years after the father died, and left the care of all the wealth and treasures in the castle to herself, telling her to make three equal parts of it, and to let herself and each of the other two sisters have one of those parts. But she was in love with a young man unknown to her father, and one night when the two sisters were fast asleep, and she thought if she killed them she would have the whole fortune for herself and her husband, she took a knife and cut their throats, and when she had them killed she got sorry and did the same to herself. The sentence put on them was that none of the three was to have rest or peace till some man without fear would come and conquer them, and John was the first to attempt this.

She took him then to her father's castle—only the ruins of it were standing, no roof and only some of the walls, and showed where all the riches and treasures were. John, to make sure, took his spade and dug away, dug with what strength was in him, and just before daybreak he came to the treasure. That moment the three sisters left good health with him, turned into three doves, and flew away.

He had riches enough for himself and for seven generations after him.

The Ghosts and the Game of Football

Patrick Kennedy

THERE WAS ONCE a poor widow woman's son that was going to look for service, and one winter's evening he came to a strong farmer's house, and this house was very near an old castle. "God save all here," says he, when he got inside the door. "God save you kindly," says the farmer. "Come to the fire." "Could you give me a night's lodging?" says the boy.

"That we will, and welcome, if you will only sleep in a comfortable room in the old castle above there; and you must have a fire and candlelight, and whatever you like to drink; and if you're alive in the morning I'll give you ten guineas." "Sure I'll be 'live enough if you send no one to kill me." "I'll send no one to kill you, you may depend. The place is haunted ever since my father died, and three or four people that slept in the same room were found dead next morning. If you can banish the spirits I'll give you a good farm and my daughter, so that you like one another well enough to be married." "Never say't twice. I've a middling safe conscience, and don't fear any evil spirit that ever smelled of brimstone."

Well and good, the boy got his supper, and then they went up with him to the old castle, and showed him into a large kitchen, with a roaring fire in the grate, and a table, with a bottle and glass, and tumbler on it, and the kettle ready on the hob. They bade him good night and Godspeed, and went off as if they didn't think their heels were half swift enough. "Well," says he to himself, "if there's any danger, this prayer-book will be usefuller than either the glass or tumbler." So he kneeled down and read a good many prayers, and then sat by the fire, and waited to see what would happen. In about a quarter of an hour, he heard something bumping along the floor overhead till it came to a hole in the ceiling. There it stopped, and cried out, "I'll fall, I'll fall." "Fall away," says Jack, and down came a pair of legs on the kitchen floor. They walked to one end of the room, and there they stood, and Jack's hair had like to stand upright on his head along with them. Then another crackling and whacking came to the hole, and the same words passed between the thing above and Jack, and down came a man's body, and went and stood upon the legs. Then comes the head and shoulders, till the whole man, with buckles in his shoes and knee-breeches, and a big flapped waistcoat and a three-cocked hat, was standing in one corner of the room. Not to take up your time for nothing, two more men, more old-fashioned dressed than the first, were soon standing in two other corners. Jack was a little cowed at first; but found his courage growing stronger every moment, and what would you have of it, the three old gentlemen began to kick a *puckeen* [football] as fast as they could, the man in the three-cocked hat playing again' the other two.

"Fair play is bonny play," says Jack, as bold as he could; but the terror was on him, and the words came out as if he was frightened in his sleep; "so I'll help *you*, sir." Well and good, he joined the sport, and kicked away till his shirt was ringing wet, savin' your presence, and the ball flying from one end of the room to the other like thunder, and still not a word was exchanged. At last the day began to break, and poor Jack was dead beat, and he thought, by the way the three ghosts began to look at himself and themselves, that they wished him to speak.

So, says he,"Gentlemen, as the sport is nearly over, and I done my best to please you, would you tell a body what is the reason of yous coming here night after night, and how could I give you rest, if it is rest you want?" "Them is the wisest words," says the ghost with the three-cocked hat, "you ever said in your life. Some of those that came before you found courage enough to take a part in our game, but no one had *misnach* [energy] enough to speak to us. I am the father of the good man of the next house, that man in the left corner is my father, and the man on my right is my grandfather. From father to son we were too fond of money. We lent it at ten times the honest interest it was worth; we never paid a debt we could get over, and almost starved our tenants and laborers."

"Here," says he, lugging a large drawer out of the wall; "here is the gold and notes that we put together, and we were not honestly entitled to the one-half of it; and here," says he, opening another drawer, "are bills and memorandums that'll show who were wronged, and who are entitled to get a great deal paid back to them. Tell my son to saddle two of his best horses for himself and yourself, and keep riding day and night, till every man and woman we ever wronged be rightified. When that is done, come here again some night; and if you don't hear or see anything, we'll be at rest, and you may marry my granddaughter as soon as you please."

Just as he said these words, Jack could see the wall through his body, and when he winked to clear his sight, the kitchen was as empty as a noggin turned upside down. At that very moment the farmer and his daughter lifted the latch, and both fell on their knees when they saw Jack alive. He soon told them everything that happened, and for three days and nights did the farmer and himself ride about, till there wasn't a single wronged person left without being paid to the last farthing.

The next night Jack spent in the kitchen he fell asleep before he was after sitting a quarter of an hour at the fire, and in his sleep he thought he saw three white birds flying up to heaven from the steeple of the next church.

Jack got the daughter for his wife, and they lived comfortably in the old castle; and if ever he was tempted to hoard up gold, or keep for a minute a guinea or a shilling from the man that earned it through the nose, he bethought him of the ghosts and the game of football.

The Brown Man
Gerald Griffin

IN A LONELY CABIN, in a lonely glen, on the shores of a lonely lough in one of the most lonesome districts of west Munster, lived a lone woman named Guare. She had a beautiful girl, a daughter named Nora. Their cabin was the only one within three miles round them every way. As to their mode of living, it was simple enough, for all they had was one little garden of white cabbage, and they had eaten that down to a few heads between them, a sorry prospect in a place where even a handful of *prishoc* weed was not to be had without sowing it.

It was a very fine morning in those parts, for it was only snowing and hailing, when Nora and her mother were sitting at the door of their little cottage, and laying out plans for the next day's dinner. On a sudden, a strange horseman rode up to the door. He was strange in more ways than one. He was dressed in brown, his hair was brown, his eyes were brown, his boots were brown, he rode a brown horse, and he was followed by a brown dog.

"I'm come to marry you, Nora Guare," said the Brown Man.

"Ax my mother fusht, if you plaise, sir," said Nora, dropping him a curtsy.

"You'll not refuse, ma'am," said the Brown Man to the old mother, "I have money enough, and I'll make your daughter a lady, with servants at her call, and all manner of fine doings about her." And so saying, he flung a purse of gold into the widow's lap.

"Why then the heavens speed you and her together, take her away with you, and make much of her," said the old mother, quite bewildered with all the money.

"Agh, agh," said the Brown Man, as he placed her on his horse behind him without more ado. "Are you all ready now?"

"I am!" said the bride. The horse snorted, and the dog barked, and almost before the word was out of her mouth, they were all whisked away out of sight. After traveling a day and a night, faster than the wind itself, the Brown Man pulled up his horse in the middle of the Mangerton mountain, in one of the most lonesome places that eye ever looked on.

"Here is my estate," said the Brown Man.

"A'then, is it this wild bog you call an estate?" said the bride.

"Come in, wife; this is my palace," said the bridegroom.

"What! a clay-hovel, worse than my mother's!"

They dismounted, and the horse and the dog disappeared in an instant, with a horrible noise, which the girl did not know whether to call snorting, barking, or laughing.

"Are you hungry?" said the Brown Man. "If so, there is your dinner."

"A handful of raw white-eyes [potatoes] and a grain of salt!"

"And when you are sleepy, here is your bed," he continued, pointing to a little straw in a corner, at sight of which Nora's limbs shivered and trembled again. It may be easily supposed that she did not make a very hearty dinner that evening, nor did her husband either.

In the dead of the night, when the clock of Muckross Abbey had just tolled one, a low neighing at the door and a soft barking at the window were heard. Nora feigned sleep. The Brown Man passed his hand over her eyes and face. She snored."I'm coming," said he, and he arose gently from her side. In half an hour after she felt him by her side again. He was cold as ice.

The next night the same summons came. The Brown Man rose. The wife feigned sleep. He returned, cold. The morning came.

The next night came. The bell tolled at Muckross, and was heard across the lakes. The Brown Man rose again, and passed a light before the eyes of the feigning sleeper. None slumber so sound as they who *will* not wake. Her heart trembled, but her frame was quiet and firm. A voice at the door summoned the husband.

"You are very long coming. The earth is tossed up, and I am hungry. Hurry! Hurry! Hurry! if you would not lose all."

"I'm coming!" said the Brown Man. Nora rose and followed instantly. She beheld him at a distance winding through a lane of frost-nipped sallow trees. He often paused and looked back, and once or twice retraced his steps to within a few yards of the tree, behind which she had shrunk. The moonlight, cutting the shadow close and dark about her, afforded the best concealment. He again proceeded, and she followed. In a few minutes they reached the old Abbey of Muckross. With a sickening heart she saw him enter the churchyard. The wind rushed through the huge yew-tree and startled her. She mustered courage enough, however, to reach the gate of the churchyard and look in. The Brown Man, the horse, and the dog, were there seated by an open grave, eating something and glancing their brown, fiery eyes about in every direction. The moonlight shone full on them and her. Looking down towards her shadow on the earth, she started with horror to observe it move, although she was herself perfectly still. It waved its black arms, and motioned her back. What the feasters said, she understood not, but she seemed still fixed in the spot. She looked once more on her shadow; it raised one hand, and pointed the way to the lane; then slowly rising from the ground, and confronting her, it walked rapidly off in that direction. She followed as quickly as might be.

She was scarcely in her straw, when the door creaked behind, and her husband entered. He lay down by her side and started.

"Uf! Uf!" said she, pretending to be just awakened, "how cold you are, my love!"

"Cold, inagh? Indeed you're not very warm yourself, my dear, I'm thinking."

"Little admiration I shouldn't be warm, and you laving me alone this way at night, till my blood is snow broth, no less."

"Umph!" said the Brown Man, as he passed his arm round her waist. "Ha! your heart is beating fast?"

"Little admiration it should. I am not well, indeed. Them praties and salt don't agree with me at all."

"Umph!" said the Brown Man.

The next morning as they were sitting at the breakfast table together, Nora plucked up a heart and asked leave to go to see her mother. The Brown Man, who ate nothing, looked at her in a way that made her think he knew all. She felt her spirit die away within her.

"If you only want to see your mother," said he, "there is no occasion for your going home. I will bring her to you here. I didn't marry you to be keeping you gadding."

The Brown Man then went out and whistled for his dog and his horse. They both came; and in a very few minutes they pulled up at the old widow's cabin-door.

The poor woman was very glad to see her son-in-law, though she did not know what could bring him so soon.

"Your daughter sends her love to you, mother," says the Brown Man, the villain, "and she'd be obliged to you for a *loand* of a *shoot* of your best clothes, as she's going to give a grand party, and the dressmaker has disappointed her."

"To be sure and welcome," said the mother; and making up a bundle of clothes, she put them into his hands.

"Whogh! whogh!" said the horse as they drove off, "that was well done. Are we to have a mail of her?"

"Easy, ma-coppuleen, and you'll get your 'nough before night," said the Brown Man, "and you likewise, my little dog."

"Boh!" cried the dog, "I'm in no hurry—I hunted down a doe this morning that was fed with milk from the horns of the moon."

Often in the course of that day did Nora Guare go to the door, and cast her eye over the weary flat before it, to discern, if possible, the distant figures of her bridegroom and mother. The dusk of the second evening found her alone in the desolate cot. She listened to every sound. At length the door opened, and an old woman, dressed in a new jock, and leaning on a staff, entered the hut. "O mother, are you come?" said Nora, and was about to rush into her arms, when the old woman stopped her.

"Whisht! whisht! my child!—I only stepped in before the man to know how you like him? Speak softly, in dread he'd hear you—he's turning the horse loose, in the swamp, abroad, over."

"O mother, mother! such a story!"

"Whisht! easy again—how does he use you?"

"Sarrow worse. That straw my bed, and them white-eyes —
and bad ones they are—all my diet. And 'tisn't that same,
only—"

"Whisht! easy, again! He'll hear you, maybe—Well?"

"I'd be easy enough only for his own doings. Listen, mother.
The fusht night, I came about twelve o'clock—"

"Easy, speak easy, eroo!"

"He got up at the call of the horse and the dog, and out a good
hour. He ate nothing next day. The second night, and the second
day, it was the same story. The third—"

"Husht! husht! Well, the third night?"

"The third night I said I'd watch him. Mother, don't hold my
hand so hard . . . He got up, and I got up after him . . . Oh, don't
laugh, mother, for 'tis frightful . . . I followed him to Muckross
churchyard . . . Mother, mother, you hurt my hand . . . I looked
in at the gate—there was great moonlight there, and I could see
everything as plain as day."

"Well, darling—husht! softly! What did you see?"

"My husband by the grave, and the horse, . . . Turn your head
aside, mother, for your breath is very hot . . . and the dog and
they eating.—Ah, you are not my mother!" shrieked the
miserable girl, as the Brown Man flung off his disguise, and
stood before her, grinning worse than a blacksmith's face
through a horse-collar. He just looked at her one moment, and
then darted his long fingers into her bosom, from which the red
blood spouted in so many streams. She was very soon out of all
pain, and a merry supper the horse, the dog, and the Brown Man
had that night, by all accounts.

The Specter Lovers
Joseph Sheridan Le Fanu

THERE LIVED SOME FIFTEEN YEARS SINCE in a small and ruinous house, little better than a hovel, an old woman who was reported to have considerably exceeded her eightieth year, and who rejoiced in the name of Alice, or popularly, Ally Moran. Her society was not much courted, for she was neither rich, nor, as the reader may suppose, beautiful. In addition to a lean cur and a cat she had one human companion, her grandson, Peter Brien, whom, with laudable good-nature, she had supported from the period of his orphanage down to that of my story, which finds him in his twentieth year. Peter was a good-natured slob of a fellow much more addicted to wrestling, dancing, and love-making, than to hard work, and fonder of whiskey punch than good advice. His grandmother had a high opinion of his accomplishments, which indeed was but natural, and also of his genius, for Peter had of late years begun to apply his mind to politics; and as it was plain that he had a mortal hatred of honest labor, his grandmother predicted, like a true fortune-teller, that he was born to marry an heiress, and Peter himself (who had no mind to forego his freedom even on such terms) that he was destined to find a pot of gold. Upon one point both agreed, that being unfitted by the peculiar bias of his genius for work, he was to acquire the immense fortune to which his merits entitled him by means of a pure run of good luck. This solution of Peter's future had the double effect of reconciling both himself and his grandmother to his idle courses, and also of maintaining that even flow of hilarious spirits which made him everywhere welcome, and which was in truth the natural result of his consciousness of approaching affluence.

It happened one night that Peter had enjoyed himself to a very late hour with two or three choice spirits near Palmerstown. They had talked politics and love, sung songs, and told stories, and, above all, had swallowed, in the chastened disguise of punch, at least a pint of good whiskey, every man.

It was considerably past one o'clock when Peter bid his companions goodbye, with a sigh and a hiccough, and lighting his pipe set forth on his solitary homeward way.

The bridge of Chapelizod was pretty nearly the midway point of his night march, and from one cause or another his progress was rather slow, and it was past two o'clock by the time he found himself leaning over its old battlements, and looking up the river, over whose winding current and wooded banks the soft moonlight was falling.

The cold breeze that blew lightly down the stream was grateful to him. It cooled his throbbing head, and he drank it in at his hot lips. The scene, too, had, without his being well sensible of it, a secret fascination. The village was sunk in the profoundest slumber, not a mortal stirring, not a sound afloat, a soft haze covered it all, and the fairy moonlight hovered over the entire landscape.

In a state between rumination and rapture, Peter continued to lean over the battlements of the old bridge, and as he did so he saw, or fancied he saw, emerging one after another along the river bank in the little gardens and enclosures in the rear of the street of Chapelizod, the queerest little whitewashed huts and cabins he had ever seen there before. They had not been there that evening when he passed the bridge on the way to his merry tryst. But the most remarkable thing about it was the odd way in which these quaint little cabins showed themselves. First he saw one or two of them just with the corner of his eye, and when he looked full at them, strange to say, they faded away and disappeared. Then another and another came in view, but all in the same coy way, just appearing and gone again before he could well fix his gaze upon them; in a little while, however, they began to bear a fuller gaze, and he found, as it seemed to himself, that he was able by an effort of attention to fix the vision for a longer and a longer time, and when they waxed faint and nearly vanished, he had the power of recalling them into light and substance, until at last their vacillating indistinctness became less and less, and they assumed a permanent place in the moonlit landscape.

"Be the hokey," said Peter, lost in amazement, and dropping his pipe into the river unconsciously, "them is the quarist bits iv mud cabins I ever seen, growing up like musharoons in the dew of an evening, and poppin' up here and down again there, and up again in another place, like so many white rabbits in a warren; and there they stand at last as firm and fast as if they were there from the Deluge; bedad it's enough to make a man a'most believe in the fairies."

This latter was a large concession from Peter, who was a bit of a free-thinker, and spoke contemptuously in his ordinary conversation of that class of agencies.

Having treated himself to a long last stare at these mysterious fabrics, Peter prepared to pursue his homeward way; having crossed the bridge and passed the mill, he arrived at the corner of the main street of the little town, and casting a careless look up the Dublin road, his eye was arrested by a most unexpected spectacle.

This was no other than a column of foot-soldiers, marching with perfect regularity towards the village, and headed by an officer on horseback. They were at the far side of the turnpike, which was closed; but much to his perplexity he perceived that they marched on through it without appearing to sustain the least check from that barrier.

On they came at a slow march; and what was most singular in the matter was that they were drawing several cannons along with them; some held ropes, others spoked the wheels, and others again marched in front of the guns and behind them, with muskets shouldered, giving a stately character of parade and regularity to this, as it seemed to Peter, most unmilitary procedure.

It was owing either to some temporary defect in Peter's vision, or to some illusion attendant upon mist and moonlight, or perhaps to some other cause, that the whole procession had a certain waving and vapory character which perplexed and tasked his eyes not a little. It was like the pictured pageant of a phantasmagoria reflected upon smoke. It was as if every breath disturbed it; sometimes it was blurred, sometimes obliterated; now here, now there. Sometimes, while the upper part was quite distinct, the legs of the column would nearly fade away or vanish outright, and then again they would come out into clear relief, marching on with measured tread, while the cocked hats and shoulders grew, as it were, transparent, and all but disappeared.

Notwithstanding these strange optical fluctuations however, the column continued steadily to advance. Peter crossed the street from the corner near the old bridge, running on tip-toe, and with his body stooped to avoid observation, and took up a position upon the raised footpath in the shadow of the houses, where, as the soldiers kept the middle of the road, he calculated that he might, himself undetected, see them distinctly enough as they passed.

"What the div—, what on airth," he muttered, checking the irreligious ejaculation with which he was about to start, for certain queer misgivings were hovering about his heart, notwithstanding the factitious courage of the whiskey bottle. "What on airth is the manin' of all this? Is it the French that's landed at last to give us a hand and help us in airnest to this blessed repale? If it is not them, I simply ask who the div—, I mane who on airth are they, for such sogers as them I never seen before in my born days?"

By this time the foremost of them were quite near, and truth to say they were the queerest soldiers he had ever seen in the course of his life. They wore long gaiters and leather breeches, three-cornered hats, bound with silver lace, long blue coats, with scarlet facings and linings, which latter were shown by a fastening which held together the two opposite corners of the skirt behind; and in front the breasts were in like manner connected at a single point, where and below which they sloped back, disclosing a long-flapped waistcoat of snowy whiteness; they had very large, long cross-belts, and wore enormous pouches of white leather hung extraordinarily low, and on each of which a little silver star was glittering. But what struck him as most grotesque and outlandish in their costume was their extraordinary display of shirt-frill in front, and of ruffle about their wrists, and the strange manner in which their hair was frizzled out and powdered under their hats, and clubbed up into great rolls behind. But one of the party was mounted. He rode a tall white horse with high action and arching neck; he had a snow-white feather in his three-cornered hat, and his coat was shimmering all over with a profusion of silver lace. From these circumstances Peter concluded that he must be the commander of the detachment, and examined him as he passed attentively. He was a slight, tall man, whose legs did not half fill his leather breeches, and he appeared to be at the wrong side of sixty. He had a shrunken, weather-beaten, mulberry-colored face, carried a large black patch over one eye, and turned neither to the right nor to the left, but rode on at the head of his men, with a grim, military inflexibility.

The countenances of these soldiers, officers as well as men, seemed all full of trouble, and, so to speak, scared and wild. He watched in vain for a single contented or comely face. They had, one and all, a melancholy and hang-dog look; and as they passed by, Peter fancied that the air grew cold and thrilling.

He had seated himself upon a stone bench, from which, staring with all his might, he gazed upon the grotesque and noiseless procession as it filed by him. Noiseless it was; he could neither hear the jingle of accoutrements, the tread of feet, nor the rumble of the wheels; and when the old colonel turned his horse a little, and made as though he were giving the word of command, and a trumpeter, with a swollen blue nose and white feather fringe round his hat, who was walking beside him, turned about and put his bugle to his lips, still Peter heard nothing, although it was plain the sound had reached the soldiers, for they instantly changed their front to three abreast.

"Botheration!" muttered Peter, "is it deaf I'm growing?"

But that could not be, for he heard the sighing of the breeze and the rush of the neighboring Liffey plain enough.

"Well," said he, in the same cautious key, "by the piper, this bangs Banagher fairly! It's either the Frinch army that's in it, come to take the town iv Chapelizod by surprise, an' makin' no noise for feard iv wakenin' the inhabitants; or else it's—it's—what it's—somethin' else. But, tundher-an-ouns, what's gone wid Fitzpatrick's shop across the way?"

The brown, dingy stone building at the opposite side of the street looked newer and cleaner than he had been used to see it; the front door of it stood open, and a sentry, in the same grotesque uniform, with shouldered musket, was pacing noiselessly to and fro before it. At the angle of this building, in like manner, a wide gate (of which Peter had no recollection whatever) stood open, before which, also, a similar sentry was gliding, and into this gateway the whole column gradually passed, and Peter finally lost sight of it.

"I'm not asleep; I'm not dhramin'," said he, rubbing his eyes, and stamping slightly on the pavement, to assure himself that he was wide awake. "It is a quare business, whatever it is; an' it's not alone that, but everything about the town looks strange to me. There's Tresham's house new painted, bedad, an' them flowers in the windies! An' Delany's house, too, that had not a whole pane of glass in it this morning, and scarce a slate on the roof of it! It is not possible it's what it's dhrunk I am. Sure there's the big tree, and not a leaf of it changed since I passed, and the stars overhead, all nght. I don't think it is in my eyes it is."

And so looking about him, and every moment finding or fancying new food for wonder, he walked along the pavement, intending, without further delay, to make his way home.

But his adventures for the night were not concluded. He had nearly reached the angle of the short lane that leads up to the church, when for the first time he perceived that an officer, in the uniform he had just seen, was walking before, only a few yards in advance of him.

The officer was walking along at an easy, swinging gait, and carried his sword under his arm, and was looking down on the pavement with an air of reverie.

In the very fact that he seemed unconscious of Peter's presence, and disposed to keep his reflections to himself, there was something reassuring. Besides, the reader must please to remember that our hero had a *quantum sufficit* of good punch before his adventure commenced, and was thus fortified against those qualms and terrors under which, in a more reasonable state of mind, he might not impossibly have sunk.

The idea of the French invasion revived in full power in Peter's fuddled imagination, as he pursued the nonchalant swagger of the officer.

"Be the powers iv Moll Kelly, I'll ax him what it is," said Peter, with a sudden accession of rashness. "He may tell me or not, as he plases, but he can't be offinded, anyhow."

With this reflection having inspired himself, Peter cleared his voice and began—

"Captain!" said he, "I ax your pardon, captain, an' maybe you'd be so condescindin' to my ignorance as to tell me, if it's plasin' to yer honor, whether your honor is not a Frinchman, if it's plasin' to you."

This he asked, not thinking that, had it been as he suspected, not one word of his question in all probability would have been intelligible to the person he addressed. He was, however, understood, for the officer answered him in English, at the same time slackening his pace and moving a little to the side of the pathway, as if to invite his interrogator to take his place beside him.

"No; I am an Irishman," he answered.

"I humbly thank your honor,' said Peter, drawing nearer — for the affability and the nativity of the officer encouraged him— "but maybe your honor is in the sarvice of the King of France?"

"I serve the same King as you do," he answered, with a sorrowful significance which Peter did not comprehend at the time, and, interrogating in turn, he asked, "But what calls you forth at this hour of the day?"

"The *day*, your honor!—the night, you mane."

"It was always our way to turn night into day, and we keep to it still," remarked the soldier. "But, no matter, come up here to my house; I have a job for you, if you wish to earn some money easily. I live here."

As he said this, he beckoned authoritatively to Peter, who followed almost mechanically at his heels, and they turned up a little lane near the old Roman Catholic chapel, at the end of which stood, in Peter's time, the ruins of a tall, stonebuilt house.

Like everything else in the town, it had suffered a metamorphosis. The stained and ragged walls were now erect, perfect, and covered with pebble-dash; windowpanes glittered coldly in every window; the green hall-door had a bright brass knocker on it. Peter did not know whether to believe his previous or his present impressions; seeing is believing, and Peter could not dispute the reality of the scene. All the records of his memory seemed but the images of a tipsy dream. In a trance of astonishment and perplexity, therefore, he submitted himself to the chances of his adventure.

The door opened, the officer beckoned with a melancholy air of authority to Peter, and entered. Our hero followed him into a sort of hall, which was very dark, but he was guided by the steps of the soldier, and, in silence, they ascended the stairs. The moonlight, which shone in at the lobbies, showed an old, dark wainscoting, and a heavy oak banister. They passed by closed doors at different landing-places, but all was dark and silent as, indeed, became that late hour of the night.

Now they ascended to the topmost floor. The captain paused for a minute at the nearest door, and, with a heavy groan, pushing it open, entered the room. Peter remained at the threshold. A slight female form in a sort of loose white robe, and with a great deal of dark hair hanging loosely about her, was standing in the middle of the floor, with her back towards them.

The soldier stopped short before he reached her, and said, in a voice of great anguish, "Still the same, sweet bird—sweet bird! still the same." Whereupon, she turned suddenly and threw her arms about the neck of the officer, with a gesture of fondness and despair, and her frame was agitated as if by a burst of sobs. He held her close to his breast in silence; and honest Peter felt a strange terror creep over him, as he witnessed these mysterious sorrows and endearments.

"Tonight, tonight—and then ten years more—ten long years—another ten years."

The officer and the lady seemed to speak these words together; her voice mingled with his in a musical and fearful wail, like a distant summer wind, in the dead hour of night wandering through ruins. Then he heard the officer say alone, in a voice of anguish—

"Upon me be it all, for ever, sweet birdie, upon me."

And again they seemed to mourn together in the same soft and desolate wail, like sounds of grief heard from a great distance.

Peter was thrilled with horror, but he was also under a strange fascination; and an intense and dreadful curiosity held him fast.

The moon was shining obliquely into the room, and through the window Peter saw the familiar slopes of the Park, sleeping mistily under its shimmer. He could also see the furniture of the room with tolerable distinctness—the old balloon-backed chairs, a four-post bed in a sort of recess and a rack against the wall, from which hung some military clothes and accoutrements; and the sight of all these homely objects reassured him somewhat, and he could not help feeling unspeakably curious to see the face of the girl whose long hair was streaming over the officer's epaulet.

Peter, accordingly, coughed, at first slightly, and afterward more loudly, to recall her from her reverie of grief; and, apparently, he succeeded; for she turned round, as did her companion, and both, standing hand in hand, gazed upon him fixedly. He thought he had never seen such large, strange eyes in all his life; and their gaze seemed to chill the very air around him, and arrest the pulses of his heart. An eternity of misery and remorse was in the shadowy faces that looked upon him.

If Peter had taken less whiskey by a single thimbleful, it is probable that he would have lost heart altogether before these figures, which seemed every moment to assume a more marked and fearful, though hardly definable, contrast to ordinary human shapes.

"What is it you want with me?" he stammered.

"To bring my lost treasure to the churchyard," replied the lady, in a silvery voice of more than mortal desolation.

The word "treasure" revived the resolution of Peter, although a cold sweat was covering him, and his hair was bristling with horror; he believed, however, that he was on the brink of fortune, if he could but command nerve to brave the interview to its close.

"And where," he gasped, "is it hid—where will I find it?"

They both pointed to the sill of the window, through which the moon was shining at the far end of the room, and the soldier said—

"Under that stone."

Peter drew a long breath, and wiped the cold dew from his face, preparatory to passing to the window, where he expected to secure the reward of his protracted terrors. But looking steadfastly at the window, he saw the faint image of a new-born child sitting upon the sill in the moonlight, with its little arms stretched toward him, and a smile so heavenly as he never beheld before.

At sight of this, strange to say, his heart entirely failed him; he looked on the figures that stood near, and beheld them gazing on the infantine form with a smile so guilty and distorted, that he felt as if he were entering alive among the scenery of hell, and shuddering, he cried in an irrepressible agony of horror—

"I'll have nothing to say with you, and nothing to do with you; I don't know what yez are or what yez want iv me, but let me go this minute, every one of yez, in the name of God."

With these words there came a strange rumbling and sighing about Peter's ears; he lost sight of everything, and felt that peculiar and not unpleasant sensation of falling softly, that sometimes supervenes in sleep, ending in a dull shock. After that he had neither dream nor consciousness till he wakened, chill and stiff, stretched between two piles of old rubbish, among the black and roofless walls of the ruined house.

We need hardly mention that the village had put on its wonted air of neglect and decay, or that Peter looked around him in vain for traces of those novelties which had so puzzled and distracted him upon the previous night.

"Ay, ay," said his grandmother, removing her pipe, as he ended his description of the view from the bridge, "sure enough I remember myself, when I was a slip of a girl, these little white cabins among the gardens by the river side. The artillery sogers that was married, or had not room in the barracks, used to be in them, but they're all gone long ago."

"The Lord be merciful to us!" she resumed, when he had described the military procession, "it's often I seen the regiment marchin' into the town, jist as you saw it last night, acushla. Oh, voch, but it makes my heart sore to think iv them days; they were pleasant times, sure enough; but is not it terrible, avick, to think it's what it was the ghost of the rigiment you seen? The Lord betune us an' harm, for it was nothing else, as sure as I'm sittin' here."

When he mentioned the peculiar physiognomy and figure of the old officer who rode at the head of the regiment—

"*That*," said the old crone, dogmatically, "was ould Colonel Grimshaw, the Lord presarve us! he's buried in the churchyard iv Chapelizod, and well I remember him, when I was a young thing, an' a cross ould floggin' fellow he was wid the men, an' a devil's boy among the girls—rest his soul!"

"Amen!" said Peter; "it's often I read his tombstone myself; but he's a long time dead."

"Sure, I tell you he died when I was no more nor a slip iv a girl—the Lord betune us and harm!"

"I'm afeard it is what I'm not long for this world myself, afther seeing such a sight as that," said Peter, fearfully.

"Nonsinse, avourneen," retorted his grandmother, indignantly, though she had herself misgivings on the subject; "sure there was Phil Doolan, the ferryman, that seen black Ann Scanlan in his own boat, and what harm ever kem of it?"

Peter proceeded with his narrative, but when he came to the

description of the house, in which his adventure had had so sinister a conclusion, the old woman was at fault.

"I know the house and the ould walls well, an' I can remember the time there was a roof on it, and the doors an' windows in it, but it had a bad name about being haunted, but by who, or for what, I forget intirely."

"Did you ever hear was there gold or silver there?" he inquired.

"No, no, avick, don't be thinking about the likes; take a fool's advice, and never go next or near them ugly black walls again the longest day you have to live; an' I'd take my davy, it's what it's the same word the priest himself I'd be afther sayin' to you if you wor to ax his raverence consarnin' it, for it's plain to be seen it was nothing good you seen there, and there's neither luck nor grace about it."

Peter's adventure made no little noise in the neighborhood, as the reader may well suppose; and a few evenings after it, being on an errand to old Major Vandeleur, who lived in a snug old-fashioned house, close by the river, under a perfect bower of ancient trees, he was called on to relate the story in the parlor.

The Major was, as I have said, an old man; he was small, lean, and upright, with a mahogany complexion, and a wooden inflexibility of face; he was a man, besides, of few words, and if *he* was old, it follows plainly that his mother was older still. Nobody could guess or tell *how* old, but it was admitted that her own generation had long passed away, and that she had not a competitor left. She had French blood in her veins, and although she did not retain her charms quite so well as Niñon de l'Enclos, she was in full possession of all her mental activity, and talked quite enough for herself and the Major.

"So, Peter," she said, "you have seen the dear, old Royal Irish again in the streets of Chapelizod. Make him a tumbler of punch, Frank; and Peter, sit down, and while you take it let us have the story."

Peter accordingly, seated near the door, with a tumbler of the nectarian stimulant steaming beside him, proceeded with marvelous courage, considering they had no light but the uncertain glare of the fire, to relate with minute particularity his awful adventure. The old lady listened at first with a smile of good-natured incredulity; her cross-examination touching the drinking-bout at Palmerstown had been teasing, but as the narrative proceeded she became attentive, and at length absorbed, and once or twice she uttered ejaculations of pity or awe. When it was over, the old lady looked with a somewhat sad and stern abstraction on the table, patting her cat assiduously meanwhile, and then suddenly looking upon her son, the Major, she said—

"Frank, as sure as I live he has seen the wicked Captain Devereux."

The Major uttered an inarticulate expression of wonder.

"The house was precisely that he has described. I have told you the story often, as I heard it from your dear grandmother, about the poor young lady he ruined, and the dreadful suspicion about the little baby. *She*, poor thing, died in that house heartbroken, and you know he was shot shortly after in a duel."

This was the only light that Peter ever received respecting his adventure. It was supposed, however, that he still clung to the hope that treasure of some sort was hidden about the old house, for he was often seen lurking about its walls, and at last his fate overtook him, poor fellow, in the pursuit; for climbing near the summit one day, his holding gave way, and he fell upon the hard uneven ground, fracturing a leg and a rib, and after a short interval died, and he, like the other heroes, lies buried in the little churchyard of Chapelizod.

The Blood-Drawing Ghost
Jeremiah Curtin

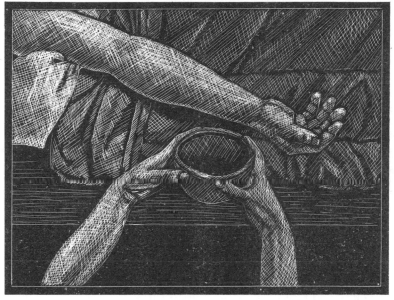

THERE WAS A YOUNG MAN in the parish of Drimoleague, county
Cork, who was courting three girls at one time, and he didn't
know which of them would he take; they had equal fortunes,
and any of the three was as pleasing to him as any other. One
day when he was coming home from the fair with his two
sisters, the sisters began:

"Well, John," said one of them, "why don't you get married?
Why don't you take either Mary, or Peggy, or Kate?"

"I can't tell you that," said John, "till I find which of them has
the best wish for me."

"How will you know?" asked the other.

"I will tell you that as soon as any person will die in the
parish."

In three weeks' time from that day an old man died. John

went to the wake and then to the funeral. While they were burying the corpse in the graveyard, John stood near a tomb which was next to the grave, and when all were going away, after burying the old man, he remained standing a while by himself, as if thinking of something; then he put his blackthorn stick on top of the tomb, stood a while longer, and on going from the graveyard left the stick behind him. He went home and ate his supper. After supper John went to a neighbor's house where young people used to meet of an evening, and the three girls happened to be there that time. John was very quiet, so that everyone noticed him.

"What is troubling you this evening, John?" asked one of the girls.

"Oh, I am sorry for my beautiful blackthorn," said he.

"Did you lose it?"

"I did not," said John; "but I left it on the top of the tomb next to the grave of the man who was buried today and whichever of you three will go for it is the woman I'll marry. Well, Mary, will you go for my stick?" asked he.

"Faith, then, I will not," said Mary.

"Well, Peggy, will you go?"

"If I were without a man forever," said Peggy, "I wouldn't go."

"Well, Kate," said he to the third, "will you go for my stick? If you go I'll marry you."

"Stand to your word," said Kate, " and I'll bring the stick."

"Believe me, that I will," said John.

Kate left the company behind her, and went for the stick. The graveyard was three miles away and the walk was a long one. Kate came to the place at last and made out the tomb by the fresh grave. When she had her hand on the blackthorn, a voice called from the tomb:

"Leave the stick where it is and open this tomb for me."

Kate began to tremble and was greatly in dread, but something was forcing her to open the tomb—she couldn't help herself.

"Take the lid off now," said the dead man when Kate had the door open and was inside in the tomb, "and take me out of this—take me on your back."

Afraid to refuse, she took the lid from the coffin, raised the dead man on her back, and walked on in the way he directed. She walked about the distance of a mile. The load, being very heavy, was near breaking her back and killing her. She walked half a mile farther and came to a village; the houses were at the side of the road.

"Take me to the first house," said the dead man.

She took him.

"Oh, we cannot go in here," said he, when they came near. "The people have clean water inside, and they have holy water, too. Take me to the next house."

She went to the next house.

"We cannot go in there," said he, when she stopped in front of the door. "They have clean water, but there is holy water as well."

She went to the third house.

"Go in here," said the dead man. "There is neither clean water nor holy water in this place; we can stop in it."

They went in.

"Bring a chair now and put me sitting at the side of the fire. Then find me something to eat and to drink."

She placed him in a chair by the hearth, searched the house, found a dish of oatmeal and brought it. "I have nothing to give you to drink but dirty water," said she.

"Bring me a dish and a razor."

She brought the dish and the razor.

"Come, now," said he, "to the room above."

They went up to the room, where three young men, sons of the man of the house, were sleeping in bed, and Kate had to hold the dish while the dead man was drawing their blood.

"Let the father and mother have that," said he, "in return for the dirty water," meaning that if there was clean water in the house he wouldn't have taken the blood of the young men. He closed their wounds in the way that there was no sign of a cut on them. "Mix this now with the meal, get a dish of it for yourself and another for me."

She got two plates and put the oatmeal in it after mixing it, and brought two spoons. Kate wore a handkerchief on her head; she put this under her neck and tied it; she was pretending to eat, but she was putting the food to hide in the handkerchief till her plate was empty.

"Have you your share eaten?" asked the dead man.

"I have," answered Kate.

"I'll have mine finished this minute," said he, and soon after he gave her the empty dish. She put the dishes back in the dresser and didn't mind washing them. "Come, now," said he, "and take me back to the place where you found me."

"Oh, how can I take you back; you are too great a load; 'twas killing me you were when I brought you." She was in dread of going from the houses again.

"You are stronger after that food than what you were in coming; take me back to my grave."

She went against her will. She rolled up the food inside in the handkerchief. There was a deep hole in the wall of the kitchen by the door, where the bar was slipped in when they barred the door; into this hole she put the handkerchief. In going back she shortened the road by going through a big field at command of the dead man. When they were at the top of the field she asked, was there any cure for those young men whose blood was drawn?

"There is no cure," said he, "except one. If any of that food had been spared, three bits of it in each young man's mouth would bring them to life again, and they'd never know of their death."

"Then," said Kate in her own mind, "that cure is to be had."

"Do you see this field?" asked the dead man.

"I do."

"Well there is as much gold buried in it as would make rich people of all who belong to you. Do you see the three *leachtans* [piles of small stones]? Underneath each pile of them is a pot of gold."

The dead man looked around for a while; then Kate went on, without stopping, till she came to the wall of the graveyard, and just then they heard the cock crow.

"The cock is crowing," said Kate; "it's time for me to be going home."

"It is not time yet," said the dead man; "that is a bastard cock."

A moment after that another cock crowed. "There the cocks are crowing a second time," said she. "No," said the dead man, "that is a bastard cock again; that's no right bird." They came to the mouth of the tomb and a cock crowed the third time.

"Well," said the girl, "that must be the right cock."

"Ah, my girl, that cock has saved your life for you. But for him I would have you with me in the grave for evermore, and if I knew this cock would crow before I was in the grave you wouldn't have the knowledge you have now of the field and the gold. Put me into the coffin where you found me. Take your time and settle me well. I cannot meddle with you now, and 'tis sorry I am to part with you."

"Will you tell me who you are?" asked Kate.

"Have you ever heard your father or mother mention a man called Edward Derrihy or his son Michael?"

"It's often I heard tell of them," replied the girl.

"Well, Edward Derrihy was my father; I am Michael. That blackthorn that you came for tonight to this graveyard was the lucky stick for you, but if you had any thought of the danger that was before you, you wouldn't be here. Settle me carefully and close the tomb well behind you."

She placed him in the coffin carefully, closed the door behind her, took the blackthorn stick, and away home was Kate. The night was far spent when she came. She was tired, and it's good reason the girl had. She thrust the stick into the thatch above the door of the house and rapped. Her sister rose up and opened the door.

"Where did you spend the night?" asked the sister. "Mother will kill you in the morning for spending the whole night from home."

"Go to bed," answered Kate, "and never mind me."

They went to bed, and Kate fell asleep the minute she touched the bed, she was that tired after the night.

When the father and mother of the three young men rose next morning, and there was no sign of their sons, the mother went to the room to call them, and there she found the three dead. She began to screech and wring her hands. She ran to the road screaming and wailing. All the neighbors crowded around to know what trouble was on her. She told them her three sons were lying dead in their bed after the night. Very soon the report spread in every direction. When Kate's father and mother heard it, they hurried off to the house of the dead men. When they came home Kate was still in bed; the mother took a stick and began to beat the girl for being out all the night and in bed all the day.

"Get up now, you lazy stump of a girl," said she, "and go to the wake-house; your neighbor's three sons are dead."

Kate took no notice of this. "I am very tired and sick," said she. "You'd better spare me and give me a drink."

The mother gave her a drink of milk and a bite to eat, and in the middle of the day she rose up.

"'Tis a shame for you not to be at the wake-house yet," said the mother; "hurry over now."

When Kate reached the house, there was a great crowd of people before her and great wailing. She did not cry, but was looking on. The father was as if wild, going up and down the house wringing his hands.

"Be quiet," said Kate. "Control yourself."

"How can I do that, my dear girl, and my three fine sons lying dead in the house?"

"What would you give," asked Kate, "to the person who would bring life to them again?"

"Don't be vexing me," said the father.

"It's neither vexing you I am nor trifling," said Kate. "I can put the life in them again."

"If it was true that you could do that, I would give you all that I have inside the house and outside as well."

"All I want from you," said Kate, "is the eldest son to marry and *Gort na Leachtan* [the field of the stone heaps] as fortune."

"My dear, you will have that from me with the greatest blessing."

"Give me the field in writing, from yourself, whether the son will marry me or not."

He gave her the field in his handwriting. She told all who were inside in the wake house to go outside the door, every man and woman of them. Some were laughing at her and more were crying, thinking it was mad she was. She bolted the door inside, and went to the place where she left the handkerchief, found it, and put three bites of the oatmeal and the blood in the mouth of each young man, and as soon as she did that the three got their natural color, and they looked like men sleeping. She opened the door, then called on all to come inside, and told the father to go and wake his sons.

He called each one by name, and as they woke they seemed very tired after their night's rest; they put on their clothes, and were greatly surprised to see all the people around. "How is this?" asked the eldest brother.

"Don't you know of anything that came over you in the night?" asked the father.

"We do not," said the sons. "We remember nothing at all since we fell asleep last evening."

The father then told them everything, but they could not believe it. Kate went away home and told her father and mother of her night's journey to and from the graveyard, and said that she would soon tell them more.

That day she met John.

"Did you bring the stick?" asked he.

"Find your own stick," said she, "and never speak to me again in your life."

In a week's time she went to the house of the three young men, and said to the father, "I have come for what you promised me."

"You'll get that with my blessing," said the father. He called the eldest son aside then and asked would he marry Kate, their neighbor's daughter. "I will," said the son. Three days after that the two were married and had a fine wedding. For three weeks they enjoyed a pleasant life without toil or trouble; then Kate said, "This will not do for us; we must be working. Come with me tomorrow and I'll give yourself and brothers plenty to do, and my own father and brothers as well."

She took them next day to one of the stone heaps in *Gort na Leachtan.* "Throw these stones to one side," said she.

They thought that she was losing her senses, but she told them that they'd soon see for themselves what she was doing. They went to work and kept at it till they had six feet deep of a hole dug; then they met with a flat stone three feet square and an iron hook in the middle of it.

"Sure there must be something underneath this," said the men. They lifted the flag, and under it was a pot of gold. All were very happy then. "There is more gold yet in the place," said Kate. "Come, now, to the other heap." They removed that heap, dug down, and found another pot of gold. They removed the third pile and found a third pot full of gold. On the side of the third pot was an inscription, and they could not make out what it was. After emptying it, they placed the pot by the side of the door.

About a month later a poor scholar walked the way, and as he was going in at the door he saw the old pot and the letters on the side of it. He began to study the letters.

"You must be a good scholar if you can read what's on that pot," said the young man.

"I can," said the poor scholar, "and here it is for you. There is a deal more at the south side of each pot."

The young man said nothing, but putting his hand in his pocket, gave the poor scholar a good day's hire. When he was gone, they went to work and found a deal more of gold in the south side of each stone heap. They were very happy then and very rich, and bought several farms and built fine houses, and it was supposed by all of them in the latter end that it was

Derrihy's money that was buried under the *leachtans*, but they could give no correct account of that, and sure why need they care? When they died, they left property to make their children rich to the seventh generation.

The Judge's House
Bram Stoker

WHEN THE TIME for his examination drew near Malcolm Malcolmson made up his mind to go somewhere to read by himself. He feared the attractions of the seaside, and also he feared completely rural isolation, for of old he knew its charms, and so he determined to find some unpretentious little town where there would be nothing to distract him. He refrained from asking suggestions from any of his friends, for he argued that each would recommend some place of which he had knowledge, and where he had already acquaintances. As Malcolmson wished to avoid friends he had no wish to encumber himself with the attention of friends' friends, and so he determined to look out for a place for himself. He packed a portmanteau with some clothes and all the books he required, and then took ticket for the first name on the local time-table which he did not know.

When at the end of three hours' journey he alighted at
Benchurch, he felt satisfied that he had so far obliterated his
tracks as to be sure of having a peaceful opportunity of pursuing
his studies. He went straight to the one inn which the sleepy
little place contained, and put up for the night. Benchurch was a
market town, and once in three weeks was crowded to excess,
but for the remainder of the twenty-one days it was as attractive
as a desert. Malcolmson looked around the day after his arrival
to try to find quarters more isolated than even so quiet an inn as
"The Good Traveller" afforded. There was only one place which
took his fancy, and it certainly satisfied his wildest ideas
regarding quiet; in fact, quiet was not the proper word to apply
to it—desolation was the only term conveying any suitable idea
of its isolation. It was an old rambling, heavy-built house of the
Jacobean style, with heavy gables and windows, unusually
small, and set higher than was customary in such houses, and
was surrounded with a high brick wall massively built. Indeed,
on examination, it looked more like a fortified house than an
ordinary dwelling. But all these things pleased Malcolmson.
"Here," he thought, "is the very spot I have been looking for,
and if I can only get opportunity of using it I shall be happy."
His joy was increased when he realized beyond doubt that it
was not at present inhabited.

From the post-office he got the name of the agent, who was
rarely surprised at the application to rent a part of the old house.
Mr. Carnford, the local lawyer and agent, was a genial old
gentleman, and frankly confessed his delight at anyone being
willing to live in the house.

"To tell you the truth," said he, "I should be only too happy,
on behalf of the owners, to let anyone have the house rent free
for a term of years if only to accustom the people here to see it
inhabited. It has been so long empty that some kind of absurd

prejudice has grown up about it, and this can be best put down by its occupation—if only," he added with a sly glance at Malcolmson, "by a scholar like yourself, who wants its quiet for a time."

Malcolmson thought it needless to ask the agent about the "absurd prejudice"; he knew he would get more information, if he should require it, on that subject from other quarters. He paid his three months' rent, got a receipt, and the name of an old woman who would probably undertake to "do" for him, and came away with the keys in his pocket. He then went to the landlady of the inn, who was a cheerful and most kindly person, and asked her advice as to such stores and provisions as he would be likely to require. She threw up her hands in amazement when he told her where he was going to settle himself.

"Not in the Judge's House!" she said and grew pale as she spoke. He explained the locality of the house, saying that he did not know its name. When he had finished, she answered:

"Aye, sure enough—sure enough the very place. It is the Judge's House sure enough." He asked her to tell him about the place, why so called, and what there was against it. She told him that it was so called locally because it had been many years before—how long she could not say, as she was herself from another part of the country, but she thought it must have been a hundred years or more—the abode of a judge who was held in great terror on account of his harsh sentences and his hostility to prisoners at Assizes. As to what there was against the house itself she could not tell. She had often asked, but no one could inform her; but there was a general feeling that there was *something*, and for her own part she would not take all the money in Drinkwater's Bank and stay in the house an hour by herself. Then she apologized to Malcolmson for her disturbing talk.

"It is too bad of me, sir, and you—and a young gentleman, too—if you will pardon me saying it, going to live there all alone. If you were my boy—and you'll excuse me for saying it—you wouldn't sleep there a night, not if I had to go there myself and pull the big alarm bell that's on the roof!" The good creature was so manifestly in earnest, and was so kindly in her intentions, that Malcolmson, although amused, was touched. He told her kindly how much he appreciated her interest in him, and added:

"But, my dear Mrs. Witham, indeed you need not be concerned about me! A man who is reading for the Mathematical Tripos has too much to think of to be disturbed by any of these mysterious 'somethings,' and his work is of too exact and prosaic a kind to allow of his having any corner in his mind for mysteries of any kind. Harmonical Progression, Permutations and Combinations, and Elliptic Functions have sufficient mysteries for me!" Mrs. Witham kindly undertook to see after his commissions, and he went himself to look for the old woman who had been recommended to him. When he returned to the Judge's House with her, after an interval of a couple of hours, he found Mrs. Witham herself waiting with several men and boys carrying parcels, and an upholsterer's man with a bed in a cart, for she said, though tables and chairs might be all very well, a bed that hadn't been aired for mayhap fifty years was not proper for young bones to lie on. She was evidently curious to see the inside of the house; and though manifestly so afraid of the "somethings" that at the slightest sound she clutched on to Malcolmson, whom she never left for a moment, went over the whole place.

After his examination of the house, Malcolmson decided to take up his abode in the great dining-room, which was big enough to serve for all his requirements; and Mrs. Witham, with the aid of the charwoman, Mrs. Dempster, proceeded to arrange matters. When the hampers were brought in and unpacked, Malcolmson saw that with much kind forethought she had sent from her own kitchen sufficient provisions to last for a few days. Before going she expressed all sorts of kind wishes; and at the door turned and said:

"And perhaps, sir, as the room is big and drafty it might be well to have one of those big screens put round your bed at night—though, truth to tell, I would die myself if I were to be so shut in with all kinds of—of 'things' that put their heads round the sides, or over the top, and look on me!" The image which she had called up was too much for her nerves, and she fled incontinently.

Mrs. Dempster sniffed in a superior manner as the landlady disappeared, and remarked that for her own part she wasn't afraid of all the bogies in the kingdom.

"I'll tell you what it is, sir," she said; "bogies is all kinds and sorts of things—except bogies! Rats and mice, and beetles; and creaky doors, and loose slates, and broken panes, and stiff drawer handles, that stay out when you pull them and then fall down in the middle of the night. Look at the wainscot of the room! It is old—hundreds of years old! Do you think there's no rats and beetles there! And do you imagine, sir, that you won't see none of them? Rats is bogies, I tell you, and bogies is rats; and don't you get to think anything else!"

"Mrs. Dempster," said Malcolmson gravely, making her a polite bow, "you know more than a Senior Wrangler! And let me say, that, as a mark of esteem for your indubitable soundness of head and heart, I shall, when I go, give you possession of this house, and let you stay here by yourself for the last two months of my tenancy, for four weeks will serve my purpose."

"Thank you kindly, sir!" she answered, "but I couldn't sleep away from home a night. I am in Greenhow's Charity, and if I slept a night away from my rooms I should lose all I have got to live on. The rules is very strict; and there's too many watching for a vacancy for me to run any risks in the matter. Only for that, sir, I'd gladly come here and attend on you altogether during your stay."

"My good woman," said Malcolmson hastily, "I have come here on purpose to obtain solitude; and believe me that I am grateful to the late Greenhow for having so organized his admirable charity—whatever it is—that I am perforce denied the opportunity of suffering from such a form of temptation! Saint Anthony himself could not be more rigid on the point!"

The old woman laughed harshly. "Ah, you young gentlemen," she said, "you don't fear for naught; and belike you'll get all the solitude you want here." She set to work with her cleaning; and by nightfall, when Malcolmson returned from his walk—he always had one of his books to study as he walked—he found the room swept and tidied, a fire burning in the old hearth, the lamp lit, and the table spread for supper with Mrs.Witham's excellent fare. "This is comfort, indeed," he said, as he rubbed his hands.

When he had finished his supper, and lifted the tray to the other end of the great oak dining-table, he got out his books again, put fresh wood on the fire, trimmed his lamp, and set himself down to a spell of real hard work. He went on without pause till about eleven o'clock, when he knocked off for a bit to fix his fire and lamp and to make himself a cup of tea. He had always been a tea-drinker, and during his college life had sat late at work and had taken tea late. The rest was a great luxury to him, and he enjoyed it with a sense of delicious, voluptuous ease. The renewed fire leaped and sparkled, and threw quaint shadows through the great old room; and as he sipped his hot tea he reveled in the sense of isolation from his kind. Then it was that he began to notice for the first time what a noise the rats were making.

"Surely," he thought, "they cannot have been at it all the time I was reading. Had they been, I must have noticed it!" Presently, when the noise increased, he satisfied himself that it was really new. It was evident that at first the rats had been frightened at the presence of a stranger, and the light of fire and lamp; but that as the time went on they had grown bolder and were now disporting themselves as was their wont.

How busy they were! and hark to the strange noises! Up and down behind the old wainscot, over the ceiling and under the floor they raced, and gnawed, and scratched! Malcolmson smiled to himself as he recalled to mind the saying of Mrs. Dempster, "Bogies is rats, and rats is bogies!" The tea began to have its effect of intellectual and nervous stimulus, he saw with joy another long spell of work to be done before the night was past, and in the sense of security which it gave him, he allowed himself the luxury of a good look round the room. He took his lamp in one hand, and went all around, wondering that so quaint and beautiful an old house had been so long neglected. The carving of the oak on the panels of the wainscot was fine, and on and round the doors and windows it was beautiful and of rare merit There were some old pictures on the walls, but they were coated so thick with dust and dirt that he could not distinguish any detail of them, though he held his lamp as high as he could over his head. Here and there as he went round he saw some crack or hole blocked for a moment by the face of a rat with its bright eyes glittering in the light, but in an instant it was gone, and a squeak and a scamper followed. The thing that most struck him, however, was the rope of the great alarm bell on the roof, which hung down in a corner of the room on the right-hand side of the fireplace. He pulled up close to the hearth a great high-backed carved oak chair, and sat down to his last cup of tea. When this was done he made up the fire, and went back to his work, sitting at the corner of the table, having the fire to his left. For a little while the rats disturbed him somewhat with their perpetual scampering, but he got accustomed to the noise as one does to the ticking of a clock or to the roar of moving water; and he became so immersed in his work that everything in the world, except the problem which he was trying to solve, passed away from him.

He suddenly looked up, his problem was still unsolved, and there was in the air that sense of the hour before the dawn, which is so dread to doubtful life. The noise of the rats had ceased. Indeed it seemed to him that it must have ceased but lately and that it was the sudden cessation which had disturbed him. The fire had fallen low, but still it threw out a deep red glow. As he looked he started in spite of his *sang froid*.

There on the great high-backed carved oak chair by the right side of the fireplace sat an enormous rat, steadily glaring at him with baleful eyes. He made a motion to it as though to hunt it away, but it did not stir. Then he made the motion of throwing something. Still it did not stir, but showed its great white teeth angrily, and its cruel eyes shone in the lamplight with an added vindictiveness.

Malcolmson felt amazed, and seizing the poker from the hearth ran at it to kill it. Before, however, he could strike it, the rat, with a squeak that sounded like the concentration of hate, jumped upon the floor, and, running up the rope of the alarm bell, disappeared in the darkness beyond the range of the green-shaded lamp. Instantly, strange to say, the noisy scampering of the rats in the wainscot began again.

By this time Malcolmson's mind was quite off the problem;

and as a shrill cock-crow outside told him of the approach of
morning, he went to bed and to sleep.

He slept so sound that he was not even waked by Mrs.
Dempster coming in to make up his room. It was only when she
had tidied up the place and got his breakfast ready and tapped
on the screen which closed in his bed that he woke. He was a
little tired still after his night's hard work, but a strong cup of
tea soon freshened him up and, taking his book, he went out for
his morning walk, bringing with him a few sandwiches lest he
should not care to return till dinner time. He found a quiet walk
between high elms some way outside the town, and here he
spent the greater part of the day studying his Laplace. On his
return he looked in to see Mrs. Witham and to thank her for her
kindness. When she saw him coming through the diamond-
paned bay window of her sanctum, she came out to meet him
and asked him in. She looked at him searchingly and shook her
head as she said:

"You must not overdo it, sir. You are paler this morning than
you should be. Too late hours and too hard work on the brain
isn't good for any man! But tell me, sir, how did you pass the
night? Well, I hope? But, my heart! sir, I was glad when Mrs.
Dempster told me this morning that you were all right and
sleeping sound when she went in."

"Oh, I was all right," he answered smiling; "the 'somethings'
didn't worry me, as yet. Only the rats; and they had a circus, I
tell you, all over the place. There was one wicked looking old
devil that sat up on my own chair by the fire and wouldn't go
till I took the poker to him, and then he ran up the rope of the
alarm bell and got to somewhere up the wall or the ceiling—I
couldn't see where, it was so dark."

"Mercy on us," said Mrs. Witham, "an old devil, and sitting
on a chair by the fireside! Take care, sir! take care! There's

many a true word spoken in jest."

"How do you mean? 'Pon my word I don't understand."

"An old devil! The old devil, perhaps. There! sir, you needn't
laugh," for Malcolmson had broken into a hearty peal. "You
young folks thinks it easy to laugh at things that makes older
ones shudder. Never mind, sir! never mind. Please God, you'll
laugh all the time. It's what I wish you myself !" and the good
lady beamed all over in sympathy with his enjoyment, her fears
gone for a moment.

"Oh, forgive me!" said Malcolmson presently. "Don't think
me rude; but the idea was too much for me—that the old devil
himself was on the chair last night!" And at the thought he
laughed again. Then he went home to dinner.

This evening the scampering of the rats began earlier; indeed
it had been going on before his arrival, and only ceased whilst
his presence by its freshness disturbed them. After dinner he sat
by the fire for a while and had a smoke; and then, having
cleared his table, began to work as before. Tonight the rats
disturbed him more than they had done on the previous night.
How they scampered up and down and under and over! How
they squeaked, and scratched, and gnawed! How they, getting
bolder by degrees, came to the mouths of their holes and to the
chinks and cracks and crannies in the wainscoting till their eyes
shone like tiny lamps as the firelight rose and fell. But to him,
now doubtless accustomed to them, their eyes were not wicked;
only their playfulness touched him. Sometimes the boldest of
them made sallies out on the floor or along the mouldings of the
wainscot. Now and again as they disturbed him Malcolmson
made a sound to frighten them, smiting the table with his hand
or giving a fierce "Hsh, hsh," so that they fled straightway to
their holes.

And so the early part of the night wore on; and despite the

noise Malcolmson got more and more immersed in his work.

All at once he stopped, as on the previous night, being overcome by a sudden sense of silence. There was not the faintest sound of gnaw, or scratch, or squeak. The silence was as of the grave. He remembered the odd occurrence of the previous night, and instinctively he looked at the chair standing close by the fireside. And then a very odd sensation thnlled through him.

There, on the great old high-backed carved oak chair beside the fireplace sat the same enormous rat, steadily glaring at him with baleful eyes.

Instinctively he took the nearest thing to his hand, a book of logarithms, and flung it at it. The book was badly aimed and the rat did not stir, so again the poker performance of the previous night was repeated; and again the rat, being closely pursued, fled up the rope of the alarm bell. Strangely too, the departure of this rat was instantly followed by the renewal of the noise made by the general rat community On this occasion, as on the previous one, Malcolmson could not see at what part of the room the rat disappeared, for the green shade of his lamp left the upper part of the room in darkness, and the fire had burned low.

On looking at his watch he found it was close on midnight and, not sorry for the *divertissement*, he made up his fire and made himself his nightly pot of tea. He had got through a good spell of work, and thought himself entitled to a cigarette; and so he sat on the great carved oak chair before the fire and enjoyed it. Whilst smoking he began to think that he would like to know where the rat disappeared to, for he had certain ideas for the morrow not entirely disconnected with a rat-trap. Accordingly he lit another lamp and placed it so that it would shine well into the right-hand corner of the wall by the fireplace. Then he got all the books he had with him, and placed them handy to throw at the vermin. Finally he lifted the rope of the alarm bell and placed the end of it on the table, fixing the extreme end under the lamp. As he handled it he could not help noticing how pliable it was, especially for so strong a rope, and one not in use. "You could hang a man with it," he thought to himself. When his preparations were made he looked around, and said complacently:

"There now, my friend, I think we shall learn something of you this time!" He began his work again, and though as before somewhat disturbed at first by the noise of the rats, soon lost himself in his propositions and problems.

Again he was called to his immediate surroundings suddenly. This time it might not have been the sudden silence only which took his attention; there was a slight movement of the rope, and the lamp moved. Without stirring, he looked to see if his pile of books was within range, and then cast his eye along the rope. As he looked he saw the great rat drop from the rope on the oak armchair and sit there glaring at him. He raised a book in his right hand, and taking careful aim, flung it at the rat. The latter, with a quick movement, sprang aside and dodged the missile. He then took another book, and a third, and flung them one after another at the rat, but each time unsuccessfully. At last, as he stood with a book poised in his hand to throw, the rat squeaked and seemed afraid. This made Malcolmson more than ever eager to strike, and the book flew and struck the rat a resounding blow. It gave a terrified squeak, and turning on his pursuer a look of terrible malevolence, ran up the chair-back and made a great jump to the rope of the alarm bell and ran up it like lightning. The lamp rocked under the sudden strain, but it was a heavy one and did not topple over. Malcolmson kept his eyes on the rat, and saw it by the light of the second lamp leap to a moulding of the wainscot and disappear through a hole in one of the great pictures which hung on the wall, obscured and invisible through its coating of dirt and dust.

"I shall look up my friend's habitation in the morning," said the student, as he went over to collect his books. "The third picture from the fireplace; I shall not forget." He picked up the books one by one, commenting on them as he lifted them. *Conic Sections* he does not mind, nor *Cycloidal Oscillations*, nor the *Principia*, nor *Quaternions*, nor *Thermodynamics*. Now for the book that fetched him!" Malcolmson took it up and looked at it. As he did so he started, and a sudden pallor overspread his face. He looked round uneasily and shivered slightly, as he murmured to himself:

"The Bible my mother gave me! What an odd coincidence." He sat down to work again, and the rats in the wainscot renewed their gambols. They did not disturb him, however; somehow their presence gave him a sense of companionship. But he could not attend to his work, and after striving to master the subject on which he was engaged, gave it up in despair, and went to bed as the first streak of dawn stole in through the eastern window.

He slept heavily but uneasily, and dreamed much; and when Mrs. Dempster woke him late in the morning he seemed ill at ease, and for a few minutes did not seem to realize exactly where he was. His first request rather surprised the servant.

"Mrs. Dempster, when I am out today I wish you would get the steps and dust or wash those pictures—specially that one the third from the fireplace—I want to see what they are."

Late in the afternoon Malcolmson worked at his books in the shaded walk, and the cheerfulness of the previous day came back to him as the day wore on, and he found that his reading was progressing well. He had worked out to a satisfactory conclusion all the problems which had as yet baffled him, and it was in a state of jubilation that he paid a visit to Mrs. Witham at

"The Good Traveller." He found a stranger in the cozy sitting-room with the landlady, who was introduced to him as Dr. Thornhill. She was not quite at ease, and this, combined with the doctor's plunging at once into a series of questions, made Malcolmson come to the conclusion that his presence was not an accident, so without preliminary he said:

"Dr. Thornhill, I shall with pleasure answer you any question you may choose to ask me if you will answer me one question first."

The doctor seemed surprised, but he smiled and answered at once, "Done! What is it?"

"Did Mrs. Witham ask you to come here and see me and advise me?"

Dr. Thornhill for a moment was taken aback, and Mrs. Witham got fiery red and turned away; but the doctor was a frank and ready man, and he answered at once and openly:

"She did, but she didn't intend you to know it. I suppose it was my clumsy haste that made you suspect. She told me that she did not like the idea of your being in that house all by yourself, and that she thought you took too much strong tea. In fact, she wants me to advise you if possible to give up the tea and the very late hours. I was a keen student in my time, so I suppose I may take the liberty of a college man, and without offense, advise you not quite as a stranger."

Malcolmson with a bright smile held out his hand. "Shake! as they say in America," he said. "I must thank you for your kindness and Mrs. Witham too, and your kindness deserves a return on my part. I promise to take no more strong tea —no tea at all till you let me—and I shall go to bed tonight at one o'clock at latest. Will that do?"

"Capital," said the doctor. "Now tell us all that you noticed in the old house," and so Malcolmson then and there told in minute detail all that had happened in the last two nights. He was interrupted every now and then by some exclamation from Mrs. Witham, till finally when he told of the episode of the Bible the landlady's pent-up emotions found vent in a shriek; and it was not till a stiff glass of brandy and water had been administered that she grew composed again. Dr. Thornhill listened with a face of growing gravity, and when the narrative was complete and Mrs. Witham had been restored, he asked:

"The rat always went up the rope of the alarm bell?"

"I suppose you know," said the Doctor after a pause, "what the rope is?"

"It is," said the Doctor slowly, "the very rope which the hangman used for all the victims of the Judge's judicial rancor!" Here he was interrupted by another scream from Mrs. Witham, and steps had to be taken for her recovery. Malcolmson having looked at his watch, and found that it was close to his dinner hour, had gone home before her complete recovery.

When Mrs. Witham was herself again she almost assailed the Doctor with angry questions as to what he meant by putting such horrible ideas into the poor young man's mind. "He has quite enough there already to upset him," she added. Dr. Thornhill replied:

"My dear madam, I had a distinct purpose in it! I wanted to draw his attention to the bell rope, and to fix it there. It may be that he is in a highly overwrought state, and has been studying too much, although I am bound to say that he seems as sound and healthy a young man, mentally and bodily, as ever I saw— but then the rats—and that suggestion of the devil." The doctor shook his head and went on. "I would have offered to go and stay the first night with him but that I felt sure it would have been a cause of offense He may get in the night some strange fright or hallucination and if he does I want him to pull that rope. All alone as he is, it will give us warning, and we may reach him in time to be of service. I shall be sitting up pretty late tonight and shall keep my ears open. Do not be alarmed if Benchurch gets a surprise before morning."

"Oh, Doctor, what do you mean? What do you mean?"

"I mean this; that possibly—nay, more probably—we shall hear the great alarm bell from the Judge's House tonight," and the Doctor made about as effective an exit as could be thought of.

When Malcolmson arrived home he found that it was a little after his usual time, and Mrs. Dempster had gone away—the rules of Greenhow's Charity were not to be neglected. He was glad to see that the place was bright and tidy with a cheerful fire and a well-trimmed lamp. The evening was colder than might have been expected in April, and a heavy wind was blowing with such rapidly-increasing strength that there was every promise of a storm during the night. For a few minutes after his entrance the noise of the rats ceased; but so soon as they became accustomed to his presence they began again. He was glad to hear them, for he felt once more the feeling of companionship in their noise, and his mind ran back to the strange fact that they only ceased to manifest themselves when that other—the great rat with the baleful eyes—came upon the scene. The reading-lamp only was lit and its green shade kept the ceiling and the upper part of the room in darkness, so that the cheerful light from the hearth spreading over the floor and shining on the white cloth laid over the end of the table was warm and cheery. Malcolmson sat down to his dinner with a good appetite and a buoyant spirit. After his dinner and a cigarette he sat steadily down to work, determined not to let anything disturb him, for he remembered his promise to the Doctor, and made up his mind to make the best of the time at his disposal.

For an hour or so he worked all right, and then his thoughts began to wander from his books. The actual circumstances around him, the calls on his physical attention, and his nervous susceptibility were not to be denied. By this time the wind had become a gale, and the gale a storm. The old house, solid though it was, seemed to shake to its foundations, and the storm roared and raged through its many chimneys and its queer old gables, producing strange, unearthly sounds in the empty rooms and corridors. Even the great alarm bell on the roof must have felt the force of the wind, for the rope rose and fell slightly, as though the bell were moved a little from time to time, and the limber rope fell on the oak floor with a hard and hollow sound.

As Malcolmson listened to it he bethought himself of the Doctor's words, "It is the rope which the hangman used for the victims of the Judge's judicial rancor," and he went over to the corner of the fireplace and took it in his hand to look at it. There seemed a sort of deadly interest in it, and as he stood there he lost himself for a moment in speculation as to who these victims were, and the grim wish of the Judge to have such a ghastly relic ever under his eyes. As he stood there the swaying of the bell on the roof still lifted the rope now and again; but presently there came a new sensation—a sort of tremor in the rope, as though something was moving along it.

Looking up instinctively Malcolmson saw the great rat coming slowly down towards him, glaring at him steadily. He dropped the rope and started back with a muttered curse, and the rat turning ran up the rope again and disappeared, and at the same instant Malcolmson became conscious that the noise of the rats, which had ceased for a while, began again.

All this set him thinking, and it occurred to him that he had not investigated the lair of the rat or looked at the pictures, as he had intended. He lit the other lamp without the shade, and, holding it up, went and stood opposite the third picture from the fireplace on the right-hand side where he had seen the rat disappear on the previous night.

At the first glance he started back so suddenly that he almost dropped the lamp, and a deadly pallor overspread his face. His knees shook, and heavy drops of sweat came on his forehead, and he trembled like an aspen. But he was young and plucky, and pulled himself together, and after the pause of a few seconds stepped forward again, raised the lamp, and examined the picture which had been dusted and washed, and now stood out clearly.

It was of a judge dressed in his robes of scarlet and ermine. His face was strong and merciless, evil, crafty, and vindictive, with a sensual mouth, hooked nose of ruddy color, and shaped like the beak of a bird of prey. The rest of the face was of a cadaverous color. The eyes were of peculiar bnlliance and with a terribly malignant expression. As he looked at them, Malcolmson grew cold, for he saw there the very counterpart of the eyes of the great rat. The lamp almost fell from his hand, he saw the rat with its baleful eyes peering out through the hole in the corner of the picture, and noted the sudden cessation of the noise of the other rats. However, he pulled himself together, and went on with his examination of the picture.

The Judge was seated in a great high-backed carved oak chair, on the right-hand side of a great stone fireplace where, in the corner, a rope hung down from the ceiling, its end lying coiled on the floor. With a feeling of something like horror, Malcolmson recognized the scene of the room as it stood, and gazed around him in an awestruck manner as though he expected to find some strange presence behind him. Then he looked over to the corner of the fireplace—and with a loud cry he let the lamp fall from his hand.

There, in the Judge's armchair, with the rope hanging behind, sat the rat with the Judge's baleful eyes, now intensified and with a fiendish leer. Save for the howling of the storm without there was silence.

The fallen lamp recalled Malcolmson to himself. Fortunately it was of metal, and so the oil was not spilt. However, the practical need of attending to it settled at once his nervous apprehensions. When he had turned it out, he wiped his brow and thought for a moment.

"This will not do," he said to himself. "If I go on like this I shall become a crazy fool. This must stop! I promised the Doctor I would not take tea. Faith, he was pretty right! My nerves must have been getting into a queer state. Funny I did not notice it. I never felt better in my life. However, it is all right now, and I shall not be such a fool again."

Then he mixed himself a good stiff glass of brandy and water and resolutely sat down to his work.

It was nearly an hour later when he looked up from his book, disturbed by the sudden stillness. Without, the wind howled and roared louder than ever, and the rain drove in sheets against the windows, beating like hail on the glass; but within there was no sound whatever save the echo of the wind as it roared in the great chimney, and now and then a hiss as a few raindrops found their way down the chimney in a lull of the storm. The fire had fallen low and had ceased to flame, though it threw out a red glow. Malcolmson listened attentively, and presently heard a thin, squeaking noise, very faint. It came from the corner of the room where the rope hung down, and he thought it was the creaking of the rope on the floor as the swaying of the bell raised and lowered it. Looking up, however, he saw in the dim light the great rat clinging to the rope and gnawing it. The rope was already nearly gnawed through—he could see the lighter color where the strands were laid bare. As he looked the job was completed, and the severed end of the rope fell clattering on the oaken floor, whilst for an instant the great rat remained like a knob or tassel at the end of the rope, which now began to sway to and fro. Malcolmson felt for a moment another pang of terror as he thought that now the possibility of calling the outer world to his assistance was cut off, but an intense anger took its place, and seizing the book he was reading he hurled it at the rat. The blow was well aimed, but before the missile could reach him the rat dropped off and struck the floor with a soft thud. Malcolmson instantly rushed over towards him, but it darted away and disappeared in the darkness of the shadows of the room. Malcolmson felt that his work was over for the night, and determined then and there to vary the monotony of the proceedings by a hunt for the rat, and took off the green shade of the lamp so as to insure a wider spreading light. As he did so the gloom of the upper part of the room was relieved, and in the new flood of light, great by comparison with the previous darkness, the pictures on the wall stood out boldly. From where he stood, Malcolmson saw right opposite to him the third picture on the wall from the right of the fireplace. He rubbed his eyes in surprise, and then a great fear began to come upon him.

In the center of the picture was a great irregular patch of brown canvas, as fresh as when it was stretched on the frame. The background was as before, with chair and chimney-corner and rope, but the figure of the Judge had disappeared.

Malcolmson, almost in a chill of horror, turned slowly round, and then he began to shake and tremble like a man in a palsy. His strength seemed to have left him, and he was incapable of action or movement, hardly even of thought. He could only see and hear.

There, on the great high-backed carved oak chair sat the

Judge in his robes of scarlet and ermine, with his baleful eyes glaring vindictively, and a smile of triumph on the resolute, cruel mouth, as he lifted with his hands a *black cap.* Malcolmson felt as if the blood was running from his heart, as one does in moments of prolonged suspense. There was a ringing in his ears. Without, he could hear the roar and howl of the tempest, and through it, swept on the storm, came the striking of midnight by the great chimes in the marketplace. He stood for a space of time that seemed to him endless stlll as a statue, and with wide-open, horror-struck eyes, breathless. As the clock struck, so the smile of triumph on the Judge's face intensified, and at the last stroke of midnight he placed the black cap on his head.

Slowly and deliberately the Judge rose from his chair and picked up the piece of the rope of the alarm bell which lay on the floor, drew it through his hands as if he enjoyed its touch, and then deliberately began to knot one end of it, fashioning it into a noose. This he tightened and tested with his foot, pulling hard at it till he was satisfied and then making a running noose of it, which he held in his hand. Then he began to move along the table on the opposite side to Malcolmson keeping his eyes on him until he had passed him, when with a quick movement he stood in front of the door. Malcolmson then began to feel that he was trapped, and tried to think of what he should do. There was some fascination in the Judge's eyes, which he never took off him, and he had, perforce, to look. He saw the Judge approach—still keeping between him and the door—and raise the noose and throw it towards him as if to entangle him. With a great effort he made a quick movement to one side, and saw the rope fall beside him, and heard it strike the oaken floor. Again the Judge raised the noose and tried to ensnare him, ever keeping his baleful eyes fixed on him, and each time by a mighty effort the student just managed to evade it. So this went on for many times, the Judge seeming never discouraged nor discomposed at failure, but playing as a cat does with a mouse. At last in despair, which had reached its climax, Malcolmson cast a quick glance round him. The lamp seemed to have blazed up, and there was a fairly good light in the room. At the many rat-holes and in the chinks and crannies of the wainscot he saw the rats' eyes; and this aspect, that was purely physical, gave him a gleam of comfort. He looked around and saw that the rope of the great alarm bell was laden with rats. Every inch of it was covered with them, and more and more were pouring through the small circular hole in the ceiling whence it emerged, so that with their weight the bell was beginning to sway.

Hark! it had swayed till the clapper had touched the bell. The sound was but a tiny one, but the bell was only beginning to sway, and it would increase.

At the sound the Judge, who had been keeping his eyes fixed on Malcolmson, looked up, and a scowl of diabolical anger overspread his face. His eyes fairly glowed like hot coals, and he stamped his foot with a sound that seemed to make the house shake. A dreadful peal of thunder broke overhead as he raised the rope again, whilst the rats kept running up and down the rope as though working against time. This time, instead of throwing it, he drew close to his victim, and held open the noose as he approached. As he came closer there seemed something paralyzing in his very presence, and Malcolmson stood rigid as a corpse. He felt the Judge's icy fingers touch his throat as he adjusted the rope. The noose tightened—tightened. Then the Judge, taking the rigid form of the student in his arms, carried him over and placed him standing in the oak chair, and stepping up beside him, put his hand up and caught the end of the swaying rope of the alarm bell. As he raised his hand the rats fled squeaking, and disappeared through the hole in the ceiling. Taking the end of the noose which was round Malcolmson's neck, he tied it to the hanging-bell rope, and then descending pulled away the chair.

* * *

WHEN THE ALARM bell of the Judge's House began to sound, a crowd soon assembled. Lights and torches of various kinds appeared, and soon a silent crowd was hurrying to the spot. They knocked loudly at the door, but there was no reply. Then they burst in the door, and poured into the great dining room, the Doctor at the head.

There at the end of the rope of the great alarm bell hung the body of the student, and on the face of the Judge in the picture was a malignant smile.

The Dead Smile
Francis Marion Crawford

I

SIR HUGH OCKRAM SMILED as he sat by the open window of his study, in the late August afternoon, and just then a curiously yellow cloud obscured the low sun, and the clear summer light turned lurid, as if it had been suddenly poisoned and polluted by the foul vapors of a plague. Sir Hugh's face seemed, at best, to be made of fine parchment drawn skin-tight over a wooden mask, in which two eyes were sunk out of sight, and peered from far within through crevices under the slanting. wrinkled lids, alive and watchful like two toads in their holes, side by side and exactly alike. But as the light changed, then a little yellow glare flashed in each. Nurse Macdonald said once that when Sir Hugh smiled he saw the faces of two women in hell—

two dead women he had betrayed. (Nurse Macdonald was a hundred years old.) And the smile widened, stretching the pale lips across the discolored teeth in an expression of profound self-satisfaction, blended with the most unforgiving hatred and contempt for the human soul. The hideous disease of which he was dying had touched his brain. His son stood beside him, tall, white, and delicate as an angel in a primitive picture, and though there was deep distress in his violet eyes as he looked at his father's face, he felt the shadow of that sickening smile stealing across his own lips and parting them and drawing them against his will. And it was like a bad dream, for he tried not to smile and smiled the more. Beside him, strangely like him in her wan, angelic beauty, with the same shadowy golden hair, the same sad violet eyes, the same luminously pale face, Evelyn Warburton rested one hand upon his arm. And as she looked into her uncle's eyes, and could not turn her own away, she knew that the deathly smile was hovering on her own red lips, drawing them tightly across her little teeth, while two bright tears ran down her cheeks to her mouth, and dropped from the upper to the lower lip while she smiled—and the smile was like the shadow of death and the seal of damnation upon her pure, young face.

"Of course," said Sir Hugh very slowly, and still looking out at the trees, 'if you have made up your mind to be married, I cannot hinder you, and I don't suppose you attach the smallest importance to my consent—"

"Father!" exclaimed Gabriel reproachfully.

"No, I do not deceive myself," continued the old man, smiling terribly. "You will marry when I am dead, though there is a very good reason why you had better not—why you had better not," he repeated very emphatically, and he slowly turned his toad eyes upon the lovers.

"What reason?" asked Evelyn in a frightened voice.

"Never mind the reason, my dear. You will marry just as if it did not exist." There was a long pause. "Two gone," he said, his voice lowering strangely, "and two more will be four—all together—for ever and ever, burning, burning, burning bright." At the last words his head sank slowly back, and the little glare of the toad eyes disappeared under the swollen lids, and the lurid cloud passed from the westering sun, so that the earth was green again and the light pure. Sir Hugh had fallen asleep, as he often did in his last illness, even while speaking.

Gabriel Ockram drew Evelyn away, and from the study they went out into the dim hall, softly closing the door behind them, and each audibly drew breath, as though some sudden danger had been passed. They laid their hands each in the other's and their strangely-alike eyes met in a long look, in which love and perfect understanding were darkened by the secret terror of an unknown thing. Their pale faces reflected each other's fear.

"It is his secret," said Evelyn at last. "He will never tell us what it is."

"If he dies with it," answered Gabriel, "let it be on his own head!"

"On his head!" echoed the dim hall. It was a strange echo, and some were frightened by it, for they said that if it were a real echo it should repeat everything and not give back a phrase here and there, now speaking, now silent. But Nurse Macdonald said that the great hall would never echo a prayer when an Ockram was to die, though it would give back curses ten for one.

"On his head!" it repeated quite softly, and Evelyn started and looked round.

"It is only the echo." said Gabriel, leading her away.

They went out into the late afternoon light, and sat upon a stone seat behind the chapel, which was built across the end of the east wing. It was very still, not a breath stirred, and there was no sound near them. Only far off in the park a song-bird was whistling the high prelude to the evening chorus.

"It is very lonely here," said Evelyn, taking Gabriel's hand nervously, and speaking as if she dreaded to disturb the silence. "If it were dark. I should be afraid."

"Of what? Of me?" Gabriel's sad eyes turned to her.

"Oh no! How could I be afraid of you? But of the old Ockrams—they say they are just under our feet here in the north vault outside the chapel, all in their shrouds, with no coffins, as they used to bury them."

"As they always will—as they will bury my father, and me. They say an Ockram will not lie in a coffin."

"But it cannot be true—these are fairy tales—ghost stories!" Evelyn nestled nearer to her companion, grasping his hand more tightly, and the sun began to go down.

"Of course. But there is a story of old Sir Vernon, who was beheaded for treason under James II. The family brought his body back from the scaffold in an iron coffin with heavy locks, and they put it in the north vault. But ever afterwards, whenever the vault was opened to bury another of the family, they found the coffin wide open, and the body standing upright against the wall, and the head rolled away in a corner, smiling at it."

"As Uncle Hugh smiles?" Evelyn shivered.

"Yes, I suppose so," answered Gabriel, thoughtfully. "Of course I never saw it, and the vault has not been opened for thirty years—none of us have died since then."

"And if—if Uncle Hugh dies—shall you—" Evelyn stopped, and her beautiful thin face was quite white.

"Yes. I shall see him laid there too—with his secret, whatever it is." Gabriel sighed and pressed the girl's little hand.

"I do not like to think of it," she said unsteadily. "O Gabriel,

what can the secret be? He said we had better not marry—not
that he forbade it—but he said it so strangely, and he smiled—
ugh!" Her small white teeth chattered with fear, and she looked
over her shoulder while drawing still closer to Gabriel. "And,
somehow, I felt it in my own face—"

"So did I," answered Gabriel in a low, nervous voice. "Nurse
Macdonald—" He stopped abruptly.

"What? What did she say?"

"Oh—nothing. She has told me things—they would frighten
you, dear. Come, it is growing chilly." He rose, but Evelyn held
his hand in both of hers, still sitting and looking up into his face.

"But we shall be married, just the same—Gabriel! Say that
we shall!"

"Of course, darling—of course. But while my father is so
very ill it is impossible—"

"O Gabriel, Gabriel dear! I wish we were married now!" cried
Evelyn in sudden distress. "I know that something will prevent
it and keep us apart."

"Nothing shall!"

"Nothing?"

"Nothing human," said Gabriel Ockram, as she drew him
down to her.

And their faces, that were so strangely alike, met and
touched—and Gabriel knew that the kiss had a marvelous savor
of evil. but on Evelyn's lips it was like the cool breath of a
sweet and mortal fear. And neither of them understood, for they
were innocent and young. Yet she drew him to her by her
lightest touch, as a sensitive plant shivers and waves its thin
leaves, and bends and closes softly upon what it wants, and he
let himself be drawn to her willingly, as he would if her touch
had been deadly and poisonous; for she strangely loved that half
voluptuous breath of fear and he passionately desired the

nameless evil something that lurked in her maiden lips.

"It is as if we loved in a strange dream," she said.

"I fear the waking," he murmured.

"We shall not wake, dear—when the dream is over it will have already turned into death, so softly that we shall not know it. But until then—"

She paused, and her eyes sought his, and their faces slowly came nearer. It was as if they had thoughts in their red lips that foresaw and foreknew the deep kiss of each other.

"Until then—" she said again, very low, and her mouth was nearer to his.

"Dream—till then," murmured his breath.

II

NURSE MACDONALD was a hundred years old. She used to sleep sitting all bent together in a great old leathern arm-chair with wings, her feet in a bag footstool lined with sheepskin. and many warm blankets wrapped about her, even in summer. Beside her a little lamp always burned at night by an old silver cup, in which there was something to drink.

Her face was very wrinkled. but the wrinkles were so small and fine and near together that they made shadows instead of lines. Two thin locks of hair, that was turning from white to a smoky yellow again, were drawn over her temples from under her starched white cap. Every now and then she woke, and her eyelids were drawn up in tiny folds like little pink silk curtains, and her queer blue eyes looked straight before her through doors and walls and worlds to a far place beyond. Then she slept again, and her hands lay one upon the other on the edge of the blanket; the thumbs had grown longer than the fingers with age, and the joints shone in the low lamplight like polished crab-apples.

It was nearly one o'clock in the night, and the summer breeze was blowing the ivy branch against the panes of the window with a hushing caress. In the small room beyond, with the door ajar, the girl-maid who took care of Nurse Macdonald was fast asleep. All was very quiet. The old woman breathed regularly, and her indrawn lips trembled each time as the breath went out, and her eyes were shut.

But outside the closed window there was a face, and violet eyes were looking steadily at the ancient sleeper, for it was like the face of Evelyn Warburton, though there were eighty feet from the sill of the window to the foot of the tower. Yet the cheeks were thinner than Evelyn's, and as white as a gleam, and her eyes stared, and the lips were not red with life, they were dead and painted with new blood.

Slowly Nurse Macdonald's wrinkled eyelids folded themselves back. and she looked straight at the face at the window while one might count ten.

"Is it time?" she asked in her little old, far-away voice.

While she looked the face at the window changed, for the eyes opened wider and wider till the white glared all round the bright violet, and the bloody lips opcncd over gleaming teeth. and stretched and widened and stretched again, and the shadowy golden hair rose and strcamed against the window in the night breeze. And in answer to Nurse Macdonald's question came the sound that freezes the living flesh.

That low moaning voice that rises suddenly, like the scream of a storm, from a moan to a wail, from a wail to a howl, from a howl to the fear-shriek of the tortured dead—he who had heard knows, and he can bear witness that the cry of the banshee is an evil cry to hear alone in the deep night. When it was over and the face was gone, Nurse Macdonald shook a little in her great chair, and still she looked at the black square of the window, but there was nothing more there. nothing but the night, and the whispering ivy branch. She turned her head to the door that was ajar, and there stood the girl in her white gown, her teeth chattering with fright.

"It is time, child." said Nurse Macdonald. "I must go to him, for it is the end."

She rose slowly, leaning her withered hands upon the arms of the chair, and the girl brought her a woolen gown and a great mantle, and her crutch-stick, and made her ready. But very often the girl looked at the window and was unjointed with fear, and often Nurse Macdonald shook her head and said words which the maid could not understand.

"It was like the face of Miss Evelyn," said the girl at last, trembling.

But the ancient woman looked up sharply and angrily, and her queer blue eyes glared. She held herself by the arm of the great chair with her left hand, and lifted up her crutch-stick to strike the maid with all her might. But she did not.

"You are a good girl," she said. "but you are a fool. Pray for wit, child, pray for wit—or else find service in another house than Ockram Hall. Bring the lamp and help me under my left arm."

The crutch-stick clacked on the wooden floor, and the low heels of the woman's slippers clappered after her in slow triplets as Nurse Macdonald got toward the door. And down the stairs each step she took was a labor in itself, and by the clacking noise the waking servants knew that she was coming, very long before they saw her.

No one was sleeping now, and there were lights and whisperings and pale faces in the corridors near Sir Hugh's bedroom, and now someone went in, and now someone came out, but everyone made way for Nurse Macdonald, who had nursed Sir Hugh's father more than eighty years ago.

The light was soft and clear in the room. There stood Gabriel Ockram by his father's bedside, and there knelt Evelyn Warburton, her hair lying like a golden shadow down her shoulders, and her hands clasped nervously together. And opposite Gabriel, a nurse was trying to make Sir Hugh drink. But he would not, and though his lips were parted, his teeth were set. He was very, very thin and yellow now, and his eyes caught the light sideways and were as yellow coals.

"Do not torment him," said Nurse Macdonald to the woman who held the cup. "Let me speak to him, for his hour is come."

"Let her speak to him," said Gabriel in a dull voice.

So the ancient woman leaned to the pillow and laid the feather-weight of her withered hand, that was like a brown moth, upon Sir Hugh's yellow fingers, and she spoke to him earnestly, while only Gabriel and Evelyn were left in the room to hear.

"Hugh Ockram," she said, "this is the end of your life; and as I saw you born. and saw your father born before you, I am come to see you die. Hugh Ockram, will you tell me the truth?"

The dying man recognized the little far-away voice he had known all his life, and he very slowly turned his yellow face to Nurse Macdonald; but he said nothing. Then she spoke again.

"Hugh Ockram, you will never see the daylight again. Will you tell the truth? "

His toad-like eyes were not dull yet. They fastened themselves on her face.

"What do you want of me?" he asked, and each word struck hollow on the last. "I have no secrets. I have lived a good life."

Nurse Macdonald laughed—a tiny, cracked laugh, that made her old head bob and tremble a little, as if her neck were on a steel spring. But Sir Hugh's eyes grew red, and his pale lips began to twist.

"Let me die in peace," he said slowly.

But Nurse Macdonald shook her head. and her brown, moth-like hand left his and fluttered to his forehead.

"By the mother that bore you and died of grief for the sins you did, tell me the truth!"

Sir Hugh's lips tightened on his discolored teeth.

"Not on earth," he answered slowly.

"By the wife who bore your son and died heartbroken, tell me the truth!"

"Neither to you in life, nor to her in eternal death."

His lips writhed, as if the words were coals between them, and a great drop of sweat rolled across the parchment of his forehead. Gabriel Ockram bit his hand as he watched his father die. But Nurse Macdonald spoke a third time.

"By the woman whom you betrayed, and who waits for you this night, Hugh Ockram, tell me the truth!"

"It is too late. Let me die in peace."

The writhing lips began to smile across the set yellow teeth, and the toad eyes glowed like evil jewels in his head.

"There is time," said the ancient woman. "Tell me the name of Evelyn Warburton's father. Then I will let you die in peace."

Evelyn started back, kneeling as she was, and stared at Nurse Macdonald. and then at her uncle.

"The name of Evelyn's father?" he repeated slowly, while the awful smile spread upon his dying face.

The light was growing strangely dim in the great room. As Evelyn looked, Nurse Macdonald's crooked shadow on the wall grew gigantic. Sir Hugh's breath came thick, rattling in his throat, as death crept in like a snake and choked it back. Evelyn prayed aloud, high and clear.

Then something rapped at the window, and she felt her hair

rise upon her head in a cool breeze, as she looked around in spite of herself. And when she saw her own white face looking in at the window, and her own eyes staring at her through the glass, wide and fearful, and her own hair streaming against the pane, and her own lips dashed with blood, she rose slowly from the floor and stood rigid for one moment, till she screamed once and fell back into Gabriel's arms. But the shriek that answered hers was the fear-shriek of the tormented corpse, out of which the soul cannot pass for shame of deadly sins, though the devils fight in it with corruption, each for their due share.

Sir Hugh Ockram sat upright in his deathbed, and saw and cried aloud:

"Evelyn!" His harsh voice broke and rattled in his chest as he sank down. But still Nurse Macdonald tortured him, for there was a little life left in him still.

"You have seen the mother as she waits for you, Hugh Ockram. Who was this girl Evelyn's father? What was his name?"

For the last time the dreadful smile came upon the twisted lips, very slowly, very surely now, and the toad eyes glared red, and the parchment face glowed a little in the flickering light. For the last time words came.

"They know it in hell."

Then the glowing eyes went out quickly, the yellow face turned waxen pale, and a great shiver ran through the thin body as Hugh Ockram died.

But in death he still smiled, for he knew his secret and kept it still, on the other side, and he would take it with him, to lie with him for ever in the north vault of the chapel where the Ockrams lie uncoffined in their shrouds—all but one. Though he was dead, he smiled, for he had kept his treasure of evil truth to the end, and there was none left to tell the name he had spoken, but there was all the evil he had not undone left to bear fruit.

As they watched—Nurse Macdonald and Gabriel, who held Evelyn still unconscious in his arms while he looked at the father—they felt the dead smile crawling along their own lips— the ancient crone and the youth with the angel's face. Then they shivered a little, and both looked at Evelyn as she lay with her head on his shoulder, and, though she was very beautiful, the same sickening smile was twisting her mouth too, and it was like the foreshadowing of a great evil which they could not understand.

But by and by they carried Evelyn out, and she opened her eyes and the smile was gone. From far away in the great house the sound of weeping and crooning came up the stairs and echoed along the dismal corridors, for the women had begun to mourn the dead master, after the Irish fashion, and the hall had echoes of its own all that night, like the far-off wail of the banshee among forest trees.

When the time was come they took Sir Hugh in his winding-sheet on a trestle bier, and bore him to the chapel and through the iron door and down the long descent to the north vault, with tapers, to lay him by his father. And two men went in first to prepare the place and came back staggering like drunken men, and white, leaving their lights behind them.

But Gabriel Ockram was not afraid, for he knew. And he went in alone and saw that the body of Sir Vernon Ockram was leaning upright against the stone wall, and that his head lay on the ground near by with the face turned up, and the dried leathern lips smiled horribly at the dried-up corpse, while the iron coffin, lined with black velvet, stood open on the floor.

Then Gabriel took the thing in his hands, for it was very light, being quite dried by the air of the vault, and those who peeped in from the door saw him lay it in the coffin again, and it rustled a little, like a bundle of reeds, and sounded hollow as it touched the sides and the bottom. He also placed the head upon the shoulders and shut down the lid, which fell to with a rusty spring that snapped.

After that they laid Sir Hugh beside his father, with the trestle bier on which they had brought him, and they went back to the chapel.

But when they saw one another's faces, master and men, they were all smiling with the dead smile of the corpse they had left in the vault, so that they could not bear to look at one another until it had faded away.

III

GABRIEL OCKRAM became Sir Gabriel, inheriting the baronetcy with the half-ruined fortune left by his father, and still Evelyn Warburton lived at Ockham Hall, in the south room that had been hers ever since she could remember anything. She could not go away, for there were no relatives to whom she could have gone, and besides there seemed to be no reason why she should not stay. The world would never trouble itself to care what the Ockrams did on their Irish estates. as it was long since the Ockrams had asked anything of the world.

So Sir Gabriel took his father's place at the dark old table in the dining room, and Evelyn sat opposite to him, until such time as their mourning should be over, and they might be married at last. And meanwhile their lives went on as before, since Sir Hugh had been a hopeless invalid during the last year of his life, and they had seen him but once a day for the little while, spending most of their time together in a strangely perfect companionship.

But though the late summer saddened into autumn, and autumn darkened into winter, and storm followed storm, and rain poured on rain through the short days and the long nights, yet Ockram Hall seemed less gloomy since Sir Hugh had been laid in the north vault beside his father. And at Christmastide Evelyn decked the great hall with holly and green boughs, and huge fires blazed on every hearth. Then the tenants were all bidden to a New Year's dinner, and they ate and drank well, while Sir Gabriel sat at the head of the table. Evelyn came in when the port wine was brought, and the most respected of the tenants made a speech to propose her health.

It was long, he said, since there had been a Lady Ockram. Sir Gabriel shaded his eyes with his hand and looked down at the table, but a faint color came into Evelyn's transparent cheeks. But, said the grey-haired farmer, it was longer still since there had been a Lady Ockram so fair as the next was to be. and he gave the health of Evelyn Warburton.

Then the tenants all stood up and shouted for her, and Sir Gabriel stood up likewise, beside Evelyn. And when the men gave the last and loudest cheer of all, there was a voice not theirs, above them all, higher, fiercer, louder—a scream not earthly, shrieking for the bride of Ockram Hall. And the holly and the green boughs over the great chimney piece shook and slowly waved as if a cool breeze were blowing over them. But the men turned very pale, and many of them sat down their glasses, but others let them fall upon the floor for fear. And looking into one another's faces, they were all smiling strangely, a dead smile, like dead Sir Hugh's. One cried out words in Irish, and the fear of death was suddenly upon them all so that they fled in panic, falling over one another like wild beasts in the burning forest, when the thick smoke runs along the flame, and the tables were overset, and drinking glasses and bottles were broken in heaps, and the dark red wine crawled like blood upon the polished floor.

Sir Gabriel and Evelyn stood alone at the head of the table before the wreck of the feast, not daring to turn to see each other, for each knew that the other smiled. But his right arm held her and his left hand clasped her right as they stared before them, and but for the shadows of her hair one might not have told their two faces apart. They listened long, but the cry came not again, and the dead smile faded from their lips, while each remembered that Sir Hugh Ockram lay in the north vault, smiling in his winding-sheet, in the dark, because he had died with his secret.

So ended the tenants' New Year's dinner. But from that time on Sir Gabriel grew more and more silent, and his face grew even paler and thinner than before. Often without warning and without words, he would rise from his seat, as if something moved him against his will, and he would go out into the rain or the sunshine to the north side of the chapel, and sit on the stone bench, staring at the ground as if he could see through it, and through the vault below, and through the white winding-sheet in the dark, to the dead smile that would not die.

Always when he went out in that way Evelyn came out presently and sat beside him. Once, too, as in summer, their beautiful faces came suddenly near, and their lids drooped, and their red lips were almost joined together. But as their eyes met, they grew wide and wild, so that the white showed in a ring all round the deep violet, and their teeth chattered, and their hands were like hands of corpses, each in the other's for the terror of what was under their feet, and of what they knew but could not see.

Once, also, Evelyn found Sir Gabriel in the Chapel alone, standing before the iron door that led down to the place of death, and in his hand there was the key to the door, but he had not put it in the lock. Evelyn drew him away, shivering, for she had also been driven in waking dreams to see that terrible thing again, and to find out whether it had changed since it had lain there.

"I'm going mad," said Sir Gabriel, covering his eyes with his hand as he went with her. "I see it in my sleep, I see it when I am awake—it draws me to it, day and night—and unless I see it I shall die!"

"I know," answered Evelyn, "I know. It is as if threads were spun from it, like a spider's, drawing us down to it." She was silent for a moment, and then she stared violently and grasped his arm with a man's strength, and almost screamed the words she spoke. "But we must not go there!" she cried. "We must not go!"

Sir Gabriel's eyes were half shut, and he was not moved by the agony on her face.

"I shall die unless I see it again," he said, in a quiet voice not like his own. And all that day and that evening he scarcely spoke, thinking of it, always thinking, while Evelyn Warburton quivered from head to foot with a terror she had never known.

She went alone, on a grey winter's morning, to Nurse Macdonald's room in the tower, and sat down beside the great leathern easy chair, laying her thin white hand upon the withered fingers.

"Nurse," she said, "what was it that Uncle Hugh should have told you, that night before he died? It must have been an awful secret—and yet, though you asked him, I feel somehow that you know it, and that you know why he used to smile so dreadfully."

The old woman's head moved slowly from side to side.

"I can only guess—I shall never know," she answered slowly in her cracked little voice.

"But what do you guess? Who am I? Why did you ask who my father was? You know I am Colonel Warburton's daughter, and my mother was Lady Ockram's sister, so that Gabriel and I are cousins. My father was killed in Afghanistan. What secret can there be?"

"I do not know. I can only guess."

"Guess what?" asked Evelyn imploringly, and pressing the soft withered hands, as she leaned forward. But Nurse Macdonald's wrinkled lids dropped suddenly over her queer blue eyes, and her lips shook a little with her breath as if she were asleep.

Evelyn waited. By the fire the Irish maid was knitting fast, and the needles clicked like three or four clocks ticking against each other. And the real clock on the wall solemnly ticked alone, checking off the seconds of the woman who was a hundred years old, and had not many days left. Outside the ivy branch beat the window in the wintry blast, as it had beaten against the glass a hundred years ago.

Then as Evelyn sat there she felt again the waking of a horrible desire—the sickening wish to go down, down to the thing in the north vault, and to open the winding-sheet, and see whether it had changed, and she held Nurse Macdonald's hands as if to keep herself in her place and fight against the appalling attraction of the evil dead.

But the old cat that kept Nurse Macdonald's feet warm, lying aways on the bag footstool, got up and stretched itself, and looked up into Evelyn's eyes, while its back arched, and its tail thickened and bristled, and its ugly pink lips drew back in a devilish grin, showing its sharp teeth. Evelyn stared at it, half fascinated by its ugliness. Then the creature suddenly put out one paw with all its claws spread, and spat at the girl, and all at once the grinning cat was like the smiling corpse far down below, so that Evelyn shivered down to her small feet and covered her face with her free hand lest Nurse Macdonald should wake and see the dead smile there, for she could feel it.

The old woman had already opened her eyes again, and she touched her cat with the end of her crutch-stick, whereupon its back went down and its tail shrunk, and it sidled back to its place in the bag footstool. But its yellow eyes looked up sideways at Evelyn, between the slits of its lids.

"What is it that you guess, Nurse?" asked the young girl again.

"A bad thing—a wicked thing. But I dare not tell you, lest it might not be true, and the very thought should blast your life. For if I guess right, he meant that you should not know, and that you two should marry, and pay for his old sin with your souls."

"He used to tell us that we ought not to marry—"

"Yes—he told you that, perhaps—but it was as if a man put poisoned meat before a starving beast, and said 'do not eat', but never raised his hand to take the meat away. And if he told you that you should not marry, it was because he hoped you would, for of all men living or dead, Hugh Ockram was the falsest man that ever told a cowardly lie and the cruelest that ever hurt a weak woman, and the worst that ever loved a sin."

"But Gabriel and I love each other," said Evelyn very sadly.

Nurse Macdonald's old eyes looked far away, at sights seen long ago, and that rose in the grey winter air amid the mists of an ancient youth.

"If you love, you can die together," she said very slowly. "Why should you live, if it is true? I am a hundred years old. What has life given me? The beginning is fire, the end is a heap of ashes, and between the end and the beginning lies all the pain in the world. Let me sleep, since I cannot die."

Then the old woman's eyes closed again, and her head sank a little lower upon her breast.

So Evelyn went away and left her asleep. with the cat asleep on the bag footstool; and the young girl tried to forget Nurse Macdonald's words, but she could not, for she heard them over and over again in the wind, and behind her on the stairs. And as she grew sick with fear of the frightful unknown evil to which her soul was bound, she felt a bodily something pressing her, and pushing her, and forcing her on, and from the other side she felt the threads that drew her mysteriously, and when she shut her eyes, she saw in the chapel behind the altar the low iron door through which she must pass to go to the thing.

And as she lay awake at night, she drew the sheet over her face, lest she should see shadows on the wall beckoning her, and the sound of her own warm breath made whisperings in her ears, while she held the mattress with her hands to keep from getting up and going to the chapel. It would have been easier if there had not been a way thither through the library, by a door which was never locked. It would be fearfully easy to take her candle and go softly through the sleeping house. And the key of the vault lay under the altar behind a stone that turned. She knew the little secret. She could go alone and see.

But when she thought of it, she felt her hair rise on her head, and first she shivered so that the bed shook, and then the horror went through her in a cold thrill that was agony again, like myriads of icy needles boring into her nerves.

IV

THE OLD CLOCK in Nurse Macdonald's tower struck midnight. From her room she could hear the creaking chains and weights in their box in the corner of the staircase, and overheard the jarring of the rusty lever that lifted the hammer. She had heard it all her life. It struck eleven strokes clearly and then came the twelfth, with a dull half stroke, as though the hammer were too weary to go on, and had fallen asleep against the bell.

The old cat got up from the bag footstool and stretched itself, and Nurse Macdonald opened her ancient eyes and looked slowly round the room by the dim light of the night lamp. She touched the cat with her crutch-stick and it lay down upon her feet. She drank a few drops from her cup and went to sleep again.

But downstairs Sir Gabriel sat straight up as the clock struck, for he had dreamed a fearful dream of horror, and his heart stood still. till he awoke at its stopping, and it beat again furiously with his breath, like a wild thing set free. No Ockram had ever known fear waking, but sometimes it came to Sir Gabriel in his sleep.

He pressed his hands on his temples as he sat up in bed, and his hands were icy cold, but his head was hot. The dream faded far, and in its place there came the sick twisting of his lips in the dark that would have been a smile. Far off, Evelyn Warburton dreamed that the dead smile was on her mouth, and awoke, starting with a little moan, her face in her hands shivering.

But Sir Gabriel struck a light and got up and began to walk up and down his great room. It was midnight, and he had barely slept an hour, and in the north of Ireland the winter nights are long.

"I shall go mad," he said to himself, holding his forehead. He knew that it was true. For weeks and months the possession of the thing had grown upon him like a disease, till he could think of nothing without thinking first of that. And now all at once it outgrew his strength, and he knew that he must be its instrument or lose his mind—that he must do the deed he hated and feared if he could fear anything, or that something would snap in his brain and divide him from life while he was yet alive. He took the candlestick in his hand, the old-fashioned heavy candlestick that had always been used by the head of the house. He did not think of dressing. but went as he was, in his silk nightclothes and his slippers, and he opened the door. Everything was very still in the great old house. He shut the door behind him and walked noiselessly on the carpet through the long corridor. A cool breeze blew over his shoulder and blew the flame of his candle straight out from him. Instinctively he stopped and looked round, but all was still, and the upright flame burned steadily. He walked on, and instantly a strong draft was behind him, almost extinguishing the light. It seemed to blow him on his way, ceasing whenever he turned, coming again when he went on—invisible, icy.

Down the great staircase to the echoing hall he went, seeing nothing but the flame of the candle standing away from him over the guttering wax, while the cold wind blew over his shoulder and through his hair. On he passed through the open door into the library. dark with old books and carved bookcases, on through the door in the shelves, with painted shelves on it, and the imitated backs of books, so that one needed to know where to find it—and it shut itself after him with a soft click. He entered the low-arched passage, and though the door was shut behind him and fitted tightly in its frame, still the cold breeze blew the flame forward as he walked. And he was not afraid, but his face was very pale, and his eyes were wide and bright, looking before him, seeing already in the dark air the picture of the thing beyond. But in the chapel he stood still, his hand on the little turning stone tablet in the back of the stone altar. On the tablet were engraved words, "*Clavis sepulchri Clarissimorum Dominorum De Ockram*"—("the key to the vault of the most illustrious lord of Ockram"). Sir Gabriel paused and listened. He fancied that he heard a sound far off in the great house where all had been so still, but it did not come again. Yet he waited at the last, and looked at the low iron door.

Beyond it, down the long descent, lay his father uncoffined, six months dead, corrupt, terrible in his clinging shroud. The strangely preserving air of the vault could not yet have done its work completely. But on the thing's ghastly features, with their half-dried, open eyes, there would still be the frightful smile with which the man had died—the smile that haunted.

As the thought crossed Sir Gabriel's mind, he felt his lips writhing. and he struck his own mouth in wrath with the back of his hand so fiercely that a drop of blood ran down his chin and another, and more, falling back in the gloom upon the chapel pavement. But still his bruised lips twisted themselves. He turned the tablet by the simple secret. It needed no safer fastening, for had each Ockram been confined in pure gold, and had the door been wide, there was not a man in Tyrone brave enough to go down to the place, saving Gabriel Ockram himself, with his angel's face and his thin, white hands, and his sad unflinching eyes. He took the great gold key and set it into the lock of the iron door, and the heavy, rattling noise echoed down the descent beyond like footsteps, as if a watcher had stood behind the iron and were running away within, with heavy dead feet. And though he was standing still, the cool wind was from behind him, and blew the flame of the candle against the iron panel. He turned the key.

Sir Gabriel saw that his candle was short. There were new ones on the altar, with long candlesticks, and he lit one and left his own burning on the floor. As he set it down on the pavement his lip began to bleed again, and another drop fell upon the stones.

He drew the iron door open and pushed it back against the chapel wall, so that it should not shut of itself while he was within, and the horrible draft of the sepulcher came up out of the depths in his face, foul and dark. He went in, but though the fetid air met him, yet the flame of the tall candle was blown straight from him against the wind while he walked down the easy incline with steady steps, his loose slippers slapping the pavement as he trod.

He shaded the candle with his hand, and his fingers seemed to be made of wax and blood as the light shone through them. And in spite of him the unearthly draft forced the flame forward, till it was blue over the black wick, and it seemed as if it must go out. But he went straight on, with shining eyes.

The downward passage was wide, and he could not always see the walls by the struggling light, but he knew when he was in the place of death by the larger, drearier echo of his steps in the greater space and by the sensation of a distant blank wall. He stood still, almost enclosing the flame of the candle in the hollow of his hand. He could see a little, for his eyes were growing used to the gloom. Shadowy forms were outlined in the dimness, where the biers of the Ockrams stood crowded together, side by side, each with its straight, shrouded corpse, strangely preserved by the dry air, like the empty shell that the locust sheds in summer. And a few steps before him he saw clearly the dark shape of headless Sir Vernon's iron coffin, and he knew that nearest to it lay the thing he sought.

He was as brave as any of those dead men had been, and they were his fathers, and he knew that sooner or later he should lie there himself, beside Sir Hugh, slowly drying to a parchment shell. But he was still alive, and he closed his eyes a moment, and three great drops stood on his forehead.

Then he looked again, and by the whiteness of the winding-sheet he knew his father's corpse, for all the others were brown with age; and, moreover, the flame of the candle was blown towards it. He made four steps till he reached it, and suddenly the light burned straight and high, shedding a dazzling yellow glare upon the fine linen that was all white, save over the face, and where the joined hands were laid on the breast. And at those places ugly stains had spread, darkened with outlines of the features and of the tight-clasped fingers. There was a frightful stench of drying death.

As Sir Gabriel looked down, something stirred behind him, softly at first, then more noisily, and something fell to the stone floor with a dull thud and rolled up to his feet; he started back, and saw a withered head lying almost face upward on the pavement, grinning at him. He felt the cold sweat standing on his face, and his heart beat painfully.

For the first time in all his life that evil thing which men call fear was getting hold of him, checking his heart strings as a cruel driver checks a quivering horse, clawing at his backbone with icy hands, lifting his hair with freezing breath climbing up and gathering in his midriff with leaden weight.

Yet presently he bit his lip and bent down, holding the candle in one hand, to lift the shroud back from the head of the corpse with the other. Slowly he lifted it.

Then it clove to the half-dried skin of the face, and his hand shook as if someone had struck him on the elbow, but half in fear and half in anger at himself, he pulled it, so that it came away with a little ripping sound. He caught his breath as he held it, not yet throwing it back. and not yet looking. The horror was working in him, and he felt that old Vernon Ockram was standing up in his iron coffin, headless, yet watching him with the stump of his severed neck.

While he held his breath he felt the dead smile twisting his lips. In sudden wrath at his own misery, he tossed the death-stained linen backward, and looked at last. He ground his teeth lest he should shriek aloud.

There it was, the thing that haunted him, that haunted Evelyn

Warburton, that was like a blight on all that came near him.

The dead face was blotched with dark stains, and the thin, grey hair was matted about the discolored forehead. The sunken lids were half open, and the candle light gleamed on something foul where the toad eyes had lived.

But yet the dead thing smiled, as it had smiled in life; the ghastly lips were parted and drawn wide and tight upon the wolfish teeth, cursing still, and still defying hell to do its worst—defying, cursing, and always and for ever smiling alone in the dark.

Sir Gabriel opened the winding-sheet where the hands were, and the blackened, withered fingers were closed upon something stained and mottled. Shivering from head to foot, but fighting like a man in agony for his life, he tried to take the package from the dead man's hold. But as he pulled at it the claw-like fingers seemed to close more tightly, and when he pulled harder the shrunken hands and arms rose from the corpse with a horrible look of life following his motion—then as he wrenched the sealed packet loose at last, the hands fell back into their place still folded.

He set down the candle on the edge of the bier to break the seals from the stout paper. And, kneeling on one knee, to get a better light, he read what was within, written long ago in Sir Hugh's queer hand.

He was no longer afraid.

He read how Sir Hugh had written it all down that it might perchance be a witness of evil and of his hatred; how he had loved Evelyn Warburton, his wife's sister; and how his wife had died of a broken heart with his curse upon her, and how Warburton and he had fought side by side in Afghanistan, and Warburton had fallen; but Ockram had brought his comrade's wife back a full year later, and little Evelyn, her child, had been born in Ockram Hall. And next, how he had wearied of the mother, and she had died like her sister with his curse on her. And then, how Evelyn had been brought up as his niece, and how he had trusted that his son Gabriel and his daughter, innocent and unknowing, might love and marry, and the souls of the women he had betrayed might suffer another anguish before eternity was out. And, last of all, he hoped that some day, when nothing could be undone, the two might find his writing and live on, not daring to tell the truth for their children's sake and the world's word, as man and wife.

This he read, kneeling beside the corpse in the north vault, by the light of the altar candle; and when he had read it all, he thanked God aloud that he had found the secret in time. But when he rose to his feet and looked down at the dead face it was changed, and the smile was gone from it for ever, and the jaw had fallen a little, and the tired dead lips were relaxed. And then there was a breath behind him and close to him, not cold like that which had blown the flame of the candle as he came, but warm and human. He turned suddenly.

There she stood, all in white, with her shadowy golden hair— for she had risen from her bed and had followed him noiselessly, and had found him reading, and had herself read over his shoulder. He started violently when he saw her, for his nerves were unstrung—and then he cried out her name in the still place of death:

"Evelyn!"

"My brother!" she answered, softly and tenderly, putting out both hands to meet his.

The Canterville Ghost
Oscar Wilde

I

WHEN MR. HIRAM B. OTIS, the American Minister, bought
Canterville Chase, every one told him he was doing a very
foolish thing, as there was no doubt at all that the place was
haunted. Indeed, Lord Canterville himself, who was a man of
the most punctilious honor, had felt it his duty to mention the
fact to Mr. Otis when they came to discuss terms.

"We have not cared to live in the place ourselves," said Lord
Canterville, "since my grandaunt, the Dowager Duchess of
Bolton, was frightened into a fit, from which she never really
recovered, by two skeleton hands being placed on her shoulders
as she was dressing for dinner, and I feel bound to tell you, Mr.
Otis, that the ghost has been seen by several living members of

my family, as well as by the rector of the parish, the Rev. Augustus Dampier, who is a Fellow of King's College, Cambridge. After the unfortunate accident to the Duchess, none of our younger servants would stay with us, and Lady Canterville often got very little sleep at night, in consequence of the mysterious noises that came from the corridor and the library."

"My Lord," answered the Minister, "I will take the furniture and the ghost at a valuation. I have come from a modern country, where we have everything that money can buy; and with all our spry young fellows painting the Old World red, and carrying off your best actors and prima-donnas, I reckon that if there were such a thing as a ghost in Europe, we'd have it at home in a very short time in one of our public museums, or on the road as a show."

"I fear that the ghost exists," said Lord Canterville, smiling, "though it may have resisted the overtures of your enterprising impresarios. It has been well known for three centuries, since I584 in fact, and always makes its appearance before the death of any member of our family."

"Well, so does the family doctor for that matter, Lord Canterville. But there is no such thing, sir, as a ghost, and I guess the laws of Nature are not going to be suspended for the British aristocracy."

"You are certainly very natural in America," answered Lord Canterville who did not quite understand Mr. Otis's last observation, "and if you don't mind a ghost in the house, it is all right. Only you must remember I warned you."

A few weeks after this, the purchase was concluded, and at the close of the season the Minister and his family went down to Canterville Chase. Mrs. Otis, who, as Miss Lucretia R. Tappan, of West 53d Street, had been a celebrated New York belle, was now a very handsome, middle-aged woman, with fine eyes, and a superb profile. Many American ladies on leaving their native land adopt an appearance of chronic ill-health, under the impression that it is a form of European refinement, but Mrs. Otis had never fallen into this error. She had a magnificent constitution, and a really wonderful amount of animal spirits. Indeed, in many respects, she was quite English, and was an excellent example of the fact that we have really everything in common with America nowadays, except, of course, language. Her eldest son, christened Washington by his parents in a moment of patriotism, which he never ceased to regret, was a fair-haired, rather good-looking young man, who had qualified himself for American diplomacy by leading the German at the Newport Casino for three successive seasons, and even in London was well known as an excellent dancer. Gardenias and the peerage were his only weaknesses. Otherwise he was extremely sensible. Miss Virginia E. Otis was a little girl of fifteen, lithe and lovely as a fawn, and with a fine freedom in her large blue eyes. She was a wonderful Amazon, and had once raced old Lord Bilton on her pony twice round the park, winning by a length and a half, just in front of the Achilles statue, to the huge delight of the young Duke of Cheshire, who proposed for her on the spot, and was sent back to Eton that very night by his guardians, in floods of tears. After Virginia came the twins, who were usually called "The Stars and Stripes," as they were always getting swished. They were delightful boys, and, with the exception of the worthy Minister, the only true republicans of the family.

As Canterville Chase is seven miles from Ascot, the nearest railway station, Mr. Otis had telegraphed for a waggonette to meet them, and they started on their drive in high spirits. It was a lovely July evening, and the air was dedicate with the scent of the pinewoods. Now and then they heard a wood-pigeon brooding over its own sweet voice, or saw, deep in the rustling fern, the burnished breast of the pheasant. Little squirrels peered at them from the beech-trees as they went by, and the rabbits scudded away through the brushwood and over the mossy knolls, with their white tails in the air. As they entered the avenue of Canterville Chase, however, the sky became suddenly overcast with clouds, a curious stillness seemed to hold the atmosphere, a great flight of rooks passed silently over their heads, and, before they reached the house, some big drops of rain had fallen.

Standing on the steps to receive them was an old woman, neatly dressed in black silk, with a white cap and apron. This was Mrs. Umney, the housekeeper, whom Mrs. Otis, at Lady Canterville's earnest request, had consented to keep in her former position. She made them each a low curtsey as they alighted, and said in a quaint, old-fashioned manner, "I bid you welcome to Canterville Chase." Following her, they passed through the fine Tudor hall into the library, a long, low room, panelled in black oak, at the end of which was a large stained glass window. Here they found tea left out for them, and, after taking off their wraps, they sat down and began to look round, while Mrs. Umney waited on them.

Suddenly Mrs. Otis caught sight of a dull red stain on the floor just by the fireplace, and, quite unconscious of what it really signified, said to Mrs. Umney, "I am afraid something has been spilt there."

"Yes, madam," replied the old housekeeper in a low voice, "blood has been spilt on that spot."

"How horrid!" cried Mrs. Otis; "I don't at all care for blood-stains in a sitting-room. It must be removed at once."

The old woman smiled, and answered in the same low,

mysterious voice, "It is the blood of Lady Eleanore de Canterville, who was murdered on that very spot by her own husband, Sir Simon de Canterville, in 1575. Sir Simon survived her nine years, and disappeared suddenly under very mysterious circumstances. His body has never been discovered, but his guilty spirit still haunts the Chase. The blood-stain has been much admired by tourists and others, and cannot be removed."

"That is all nonsense," cried Washington Otis; "Pinkerton's Champion Stain Remover and Paragon Detergent will clean it up in no time," and before the terrified housekeeper could interfere, he had fallen upon his knees and was rapidly scouring the floor with a small stick of what looked like a black cosmetic. In a few moments no trace of the blood-stain could be seen.

"I knew Pinkerton would do it," he exclaimed, triumphantly, as he looked round at his admiring family; but no sooner had he said these words than a terrible flash of lightning lit up the sombre room, a fearful peal of thunder made them all start to their feet, and Mrs. Umney fainted.

"What a monstrous climate!" said the American Minister, calmly, as he lit a long cheroot. "I guess the old country is so overpopulated that they have not enough decent weather for everybody. I have always been of opinion that emigration is the only thing for England."

"My dear Hiram," cried Mrs. Otis, "what can we do with a woman who faints?"

"Charge it to her like breakages," answered the Minister; "she won't faint after that"; and in a few moments Mrs. Umney certainly came to. There was no doubt, however, that she was extremly upset, and she sternly warned Mr. Otis to beware of some trouble coming to the house.

"I have seen things with my own eyes, sir," she said, "that

would make any Christian's hair stand on end, and many and many a night I have not closed my eyes in sleep for the awful things that are done here." Mr. Otis, however, and his wife warmly assured the honest soul that they were not afraid of ghosts, and, after invoking the blessings of Providence on her new master and mistress, and making arrangements for an increase of salary, the old housekeeper tottered off to her own room.

II

THE STORM raged fiercely all that night, but nothing of particular note occurred. The next morning, however, when they came down to breakfast, they found the terrible stain of blood once again on the floor. "I don't think it can be the fault of the Paragon Detergent," said Washington, "for I have tried it with everything. It must be the ghost." He accordingly rubbed out the stain a second time, but the second morning it appeared again. The third morning also it was there, though the library had been locked up at night by Mr. Otis himself, and the key carried upstairs. The whole family were now quite interested; Mr. Otis began to suspect that he had been too dogmatic in his denial of the existence of ghosts, Mrs. Otis expressed her intention of joining the Psychical Society, and Washington prepared a long letter to Messrs. Myers and Podmore on the subject of the Permanence of Sanguineous Stains when connected with Crime. That night all doubts about the objective existence of phantasmata were removed for ever.

The day had been warm and sunny; and, in the cool of the evening, the whole family went out to drive. They did not return home till nine o'clock, when they had a light supper. The conversation in no way turned upon ghosts, so there were not even those primary conditions of receptive expectations which so often precede the presentation of psychical phenomena. The subjects discussed, as I have since learned from Mr. Otis, were merely such as form the ordinary conversation of cultured Americans of the better class, such as the immense superiority of Miss Fanny Devonport over Sarah Bernhardt as an actress; the difficulty of obtaining green corn, buckwheat cakes, and hominy, even in the best English houses; the importance of Boston in the development of the world-soul; the advantages of the baggage-check system in railway travelling; and the sweetness of the New York accent as compared to the London drawl. No mention at all was made of the supernatural, nor was

Sir Simon de Canterville alluded to in any way. At eleven o'clock the family retired, and by half-past all the lights were out. Some time after, Mr. Otis was awakened by a curious noise in the corridor, outside his room. It sounded like the clank of metal, and seemed to be coming nearer every moment. He got up at once, struck a match, and looked at the time. It was exactly one o'clock. He was quite calm, and felt his pulse, which was not at all feverish. The strange noise still continued, and with it he heard distinctly the sound of footsteps. He put on his slippers, took a small oblong phial out of his dressing-case, and opened the door. Right in front of him he saw, in the wan moonlight, an old man of terrible aspect. His eyes were as red burning coals; long grey hair fell over his shoulders in matted coils; his garments, which were of antique cut, were soiled and ragged, and from his wrists and ankles hung heavy manacles and rusty gyves.

"My dear sir," said Mr. Otis, "I really must insist on your oiling those chains, and have brought you for that purpose a small bottle of the Tammany Rising Sun Lubricator. It is said to be completely efficacious upon one application, and there are several testimonials to that effect on the wrapper from some of our most eminent native divines. I shall leave it here for you by the bedroom candles, and will be happy to supply you with more, should you require it." With these words the United States Minister laid the bottle down on a marble table, and, closing his door, retired to rest.

For a moment the Canterville ghost stood quite motionless in natural indignation; then, dashing the bottle violently upon the polished floor, he fled down the corridor, uttering hollow groans, and emitting a ghastly green light. Just, however, as he reached the top of the great oak staircase, a door was flung open, two little white-robed figures appeared, and a large pillow whizzed past his head! There was evidently no time to be lost, so, hastily adopting the Fourth dimension of Space as a means of escape, he vanished through the wainscoting, and the house became quite quiet.

On reaching a small secret chamber in the left wing, he leaned up against a moonbeam to recover his breath, and began to try and realize his position. Never in a brilliant and uninterrupted career of three hundred years, had he been so grossly insulted. He thought of the Dowager Duchess, whom he had frightened into a fit as she stood before the glass in her lace and diamonds; of the four housemaids, who had gone into hysterics when he merely grinned at them through the curtains on one of the spare bedrooms; of the rector of the parish, whose candle he had blown out as he was coming late one night from the library, and who had been under the care of Sir William Gull ever since, a perfect martyr to nervous disorders; and of old Madame de Tremouillac, who, having wakened up one morning early and seen a skeleton seated in an armchair by the fire reading her diary, had been confined to her bed for six weeks with an attack of brain fever, and, on her recovery, had become reconciled to the Church, and broken off her connection with that notorious sceptic, Monsieur de Voltaire. He remembered the terrible night when the wicked Lord Canterville was found choking in his dressing-room, with the knave of diamonds half-way down his throat, and confessed, just before he died, that he had cheated Charles James Fox out of £50,000 at Crockford's by means of that very card, and swore that the ghost had made him swallow it. All his great achievements came back to him again, from the butler who had shot himself in the pantry because he had seen a green hand tapping at the window-pane, to the beautiful Lady Stutfield, who was always obliged to wear a black velvet band round her throat to hide the mark of five fingers burnt upon her white skin, and who drowned herself at last in the carp-pond at the end of the King's Walk. With the enthusiastic egotism of the true artist, he went over his most celebrated performances, and smiled bitterly to himself as he recalled to mind his last appearance as "Red Reuben, or the Strangled Babe," his *début* as "Gaunt Gibeon, the Blood-sucker of Bexley Moor," and the *furore* he had excited one lovely June evening by merely playing ninepins with his own bones upon the lawn-tennis ground. And after all this some wretched modern Americans were to come and offer him the Rising Sun Lubricator, and throw pillows at his head! It was quite unbearable. Besides, no ghost in history had ever been treated in this manner. Accordingly, he determined to have vengeance, and remained till daylight in an attitude of deep thought.

III

THE next morning, when the Otis family met at breakfast, they discussed the ghost at some length. The United States Minister was naturally a little annoyed to find that his present had not been accepted. "I have no wish," he said, "to do the ghost any personal injury, and I must say that, considering the length of time he has been in the house I don't think it is at all polite to throw pillows at him"—a very just remark, at which, I am sorry to say, the twins burst into shouts of laughter. "Upon the other hand," he continued, "if he really declines to use the Rising Sun Lubricator, we shall have to take his chains from him. It would be quite impossible to sleep, with such a noise going on outside the bedrooms."

For the rest of the week, however, they were undisturbed, the only thing that excited any attention being the continual renewal of the blood-stain on the library floor. This certainly was very strange, as the door was always locked at night by Mr. Otis, and the windows kept closely barred. The chameleon-like color, also, of the stain excited a good deal of comment. Some mornings it was a dull (almost Indian) red, then it would be vermillion, then a rich purple, and once when they came down for family prayers, according to the simple rites of the Free American Reformed Episcopalian Church, they found it a bright emerald-green. These kaleidoscopic changes naturally amused the party very much, and bets on the subject were freely made every evening. The only person who did not enter into the joke was little Virginia, who, for some unexplained reason, was always a good deal distressed at the sight of the blood-stain, and very nearly cried the morning it was emerald-green.

The second appearance of the ghost was on Sunday night. Shortly after they had gone to bed they were suddenly alarmed by a fearful crash in the hall. Rushing down-stairs, they found that a large suit of old armor had become detached from its stand, and had fallen on the stone floor, while seated in a high-backed chair was the Canterville ghost, rubbing his knees with an expression of acute agony on his face. The twins, having brought their pea-shooters with them, at once discharged two pellets on him, with that accuracy of aim which can only be attained by long and careful practice on a writing-master, while the United States Minister covered him with his revolver, and called upon him, in accordance with Californian etiquette, to hold up his hands! The ghost started up with a wild shriek of rage, and swept through them like a mist, extinguishing Washington Otis's candle as he passed, and so leaving them all in total darkness. On reaching the top of the staircase he recovered himself, and determined to give his celebrated peal of demoniac laughter. This he had on more than one occasion found extremely useful. It was said to have turned Lord Raker's wig grey in a single night, and had certainly made three of Lady Canterville's French governesses give warning before their month was up. He accordingly laughed his most horrible laugh, till the old vaulted roof rang and rang again, but hardly had the fearful echo died away when a door opened, and Mrs. Otis came out in a light blue dressing-gown. "I am afraid you are far from well," she said, "and have brought you a bottle of Doctor Dobell's tincture. If it is indigestion, you will find it a most excellent remedy." The ghost glared at her in fury, and began at once to make preparations for turning himself into a large black dog, an accomplishment for which he was justly renowned, and to which the family doctor always attributed the permanent idiocy of Lord Canterville's uncle, the Hon. Thomas Horton. The sound of approaching footsteps, however, made him hesitate in his fell purpose, so he contented himself with becoming faintly phosphorescent, and vanished with a deep churchyard groan, just as the twins had come up to him.

On reaching his room he entirely broke down, and became a prey to the most violent agitation. The vulgarity of the twins, and the gross materialism of Mrs. Otis, were naturally extremely annoying, but what really distressed him most was that he had been unable to wear the suit of mail. He had hoped that even modern Americans would be thrilled by the sight of a Spectre in Armor, if for no more sensible reason, at least out of respect for their national poet Longfellow, over whose graceful and attractive poetry he himself had whiled away many a weary hour when the Cantervilles were up in town. Besides it was his own suit. He had worn it with great success at the Kenilworth tournament, and had been highly complimented on it by no less a person than the Virgin Queen herself. Yet when he had put it on, he had been completely overpowered by the weight of the huge breastplate and steel casque, and had fallen heavily on the stone pavement, barking both his knees severely, and bruising the knuckles of his right hand.

For some days after this he was extremely ill, and hardly stirred out of his room at all, except to keep the blood-stain in proper repair. However, by taking great care of himself, he recovered, and resolved to make a third attempt to frighten the United States Minister and his family. He selected Friday, August 17th, for his appearance, and spent most of that day in looking over his wardrobe, ultimately deciding in favor of a large slouched hat with a red feather, a winding-sheet frilled at the wrists and neck, and a rusty dagger. Towards evening a violent storm of rain came on, and the wind was so high that all the windows and doors in the old house shook and rattled. In fact, it was just such weather as he loved. His plan of action was this. He was to make his way quietly to Washington Otis's room, gibber at him from the foot of the bed, and stab himself three times in the throat to the sound of low music. He bore Washington a special grudge, being quite aware that it was he who was in the habit of removing the famous Canterville blood-stain by means of Pinkerton's Paragon Detergent. Having reduced the reckless and foolhardy youth to a condition of abject terror, he was then to proceed to the room occupied by the United States Minister and his wife, and there to place a clammy hand on Mrs. Otis's forehead, while he hissed into her trembling husband's ear the awful secrets of the charnel-house. With regard to little Virginia, he had not quite made up his mind. She had never insulted him in any way, and was pretty and gentle. A few hollow groans from the wardrobe, he thought, would be more than sufficient, or, if that failed to wake her, he might grabble at the counterpane with palsy-twitching fingers. As for the twins, he was quite determined to teach them a lesson. The first thing to be done was, of course, to sit upon their chests, so as to produce the stifling sensation of nightmare. Then, as their beds were quite close to each other, to stand between them in the form of a green, icy-cold corpse, till they became paralyzed with fear, and finally, to throw off the winding-sheet, and crawl round the room, with white, bleached bones and one rolling eyeball, in the character of "Dumb Daniel, or the Suicide's Skeleton," a *rôle* in which he had on more than one occasion produced a great effect, and which he considered quite equal to his famous part of "Martin the Maniac, or the Masked Mystery." At half-past ten he heard the family going to bed. For some time he was disturbed by wild shrieks of laughter from the twins, who, with the light-hearted gaiety of schoolboys, were evidently amusing themselves before they retired to rest, but at a quarter-past eleven all was still and as midnight sounded, he sallied forth. The owl beat against the windowpanes, the raven croaked from the old yew-tree, and the wind wandered moaning round the house like a lost soul; but the Otis family slept unconscious of their doom, and high above the rain and storm he could hear the steady snoring of the Minister for the United States. He stepped stealthily out of the wainscoting, with an evil smile on his cruel, wrinkled mouth, and the moon hid her face in a cloud as he stole past the great oriel window, where his own arms and those of his murdered wife were blazoned in azure and gold. On and on he glided, like an evil shadow, the very darkness seeming to loathe him as he passed. Once he thought he heard something call, and stopped; but it was only the baying of a dog from the Red Farm, and he went on muttering strange sixteenth-century curses, and ever and anon brandishing the rusty dagger in the midnight air. Finally he reached the corner of the passage that led to luckless Washington's room. For a moment he paused there, the wind blowing his long grey locks about his head, and twisting into grotesque and fantastic folds the nameless horror of the dead man's shroud. Then the clock struck the quarter, and he felt the time was come. He chuckled to himself, and turned the corner; but no sooner had he done so than, with a piteous wail of terror, he fell back, and hid his blanched face in his long, bony hands. Right in front of him was standing a horrible spectre, motionless as a carven image, and monstrous as a madman's dream! Its head was bald and burnished; its face round, and fat, and white; and hideous laughter seemed to have writhed its features into an eternal grin. From the eyes streamed rays of scarlet light, the mouth was a wide well of fire, and a hideous garment, like to his own, swathed with its silent snows the Titan form. On its breast was a placard with strange writing in antique characters, some scroll of shame it seemed, some record of wild sins, some awful calendar of crime, and, with its right hand, it bore aloft a falchion of gleaming steel.

Never having seen a ghost before, he naturally was terribly frightened, and, after a second hasty glance at the awful phantom, he fled back to his room, tripping up in his long winding-sheet as he sped down the corridor, and finally dropping the rusty dagger into the Minister's jackboots, where it was found in the morning by the butler. Once in the privacy of his own apartment, he flung himself down on a small pallet-bed, and hid his face under the clothes. After a time, however, the brave old Canterville spirit asserted itself, and he determined to go and speak to the other ghost as soon as it was daylight. Accordingly, just as the dawn was touching the hills with silver, he returned towards the spot where he had first laid eyes on the grisly phantom, feeling that, after all, two ghosts were better than one, and that, by the aid of his new friend, he might safely grapple with the twins. On reaching the spot, however, a terrible sight met his gaze. Something had evidently happened to the spectre, for the light had entirely faded from its hollow eyes, the gleaming falchion had fallen from its hand, and it was leaning up against the wall in a strained and uncomfortable attitude. He rushed forward and seized it in his arms, when, to his horror, the head slipped off and rolled on the floor, the body assumed a recumbent posture, and he found himself clasping a white dimity bed-curtain, with a sweeping brush, a kitchen cleaver, and a hollow turnip lying at his feet! Unable to understand this curious transformation, he clutched the placard with feverish haste, and there, in the grey morning light, he read these fearful words:—

YE OTIS GHOSTE
Ye Onlie True and Originale Spook
Beware of Ye Imitationes.
All others are counterfeite.

The whole thing flashed across him. He had been tricked, foiled, and outwitted! The old Canterville look came into his eyes; he ground his toothless gums together; and, raising his withered hands high above his head, swore according to the picturesque phraseology of the antique school, that, when

Chanticleer had sounded twice his merry horn, deeds of blood would be wrought, and murder walk abroad with silent feet.

Hardly had he finished this awful oath when, from the red-tiled roof of a distant homestead, a cock crew. He laughed a long, low, bitter laugh, and waited. Hour after hour he waited, but the cock, for some strange reason, did not crow again. Finally, at half-past seven, the arrival of the housemaids made him give up his fearful vigil, and he stalked back to his room, thinking of his vain oath and baffled purpose. There he consulted several books of ancient chivalry, of which he was exceedingly fond, and found that, on every occasion on which this oath had been used, Chanticleer had always crowed a second time. "Perdition seize the naughty fowl," he muttered, "I have seen the day when, with my stout spear, I would have run him through the gorge, and made him crow for me as 'twere in death!" He then retired to a comfortable lead coffin, and stayed there till evening.

IV

THE next day the ghost was very weak and tired. The terrible excitement of the last four weeks was beginning to have its effect. His nerves were completely shattered, and he started at the slightest noise. For five days he kept to his room, and at last made up his mind to give up the point of the blood-stain on the library floor. If the Otis family did not want it, they clearly did not deserve it. They were evidently people on a low, material plane of existence, and quite incapable of appreciating the symbolic value of sensuous phenomena. The question of phantasmic apparitions, and the development of astral bodies, was of course quite a different matter, and really not under his control. It was his solemn duty to appear in the corridor once a week, and to gibber from the large oriel window on the first and third Wednesdays in every month, and he did not see how he could honorably escape from his obligations. It is quite true that his life had been very evil, but, upon the other hand, he was most conscientious in all things connected with the supernatural. For the next three Saturdays, accordingly, he traversed the corridor as usual between midnight and three o'clock, taking every possible precaution against being either heard or seen. He removed his boots, trod as lightly as possible on the old worm-eaten boards, wore a large black velvet cloak, and was careful to use the Rising Sun Lubricator for oiling his chains. I am bound to acknowledge that it was with a good deal of difficulty that he brought himself to adopt this last mode of protection. However, one night, while the family were at dinner, he slipped into Mr. Otis's bedroom and carried off the bottle. He felt a little humiliated at first, but afterwards was sensible enough to see that there was a great deal to be said for the invention, and, to a certain degree, it served his purpose. Still, in spite of everything he was not left unmolested. Strings were continually being stretched across the corridor, over which he tripped in the dark, and on one occasion, while dressed for the part of "Black Isaac, or the Huntsman of Hogley Woods," he met with a severe fall, through treading on a butter-slide, which the twins had constructed from the entrance of the Tapestry Chamber to the top of the oak staircase. This last insult so enraged him, that he resolved to make one final effort to assert his dignity and social position, and determined to visit the insolent young Etonians the next night in his celebrated character of "Reckless Rupert, or the Headless Earl."

He had not appeared in this disguise for more than seventy years; in fact, not since he had so frightened pretty Lady Barbara Modish by means of it, that she suddenly broke off her engagement with the present Lord Canterville's grandfather, and ran away to Gretna Green with handsome Jack Castletown, declaring that nothing in the world would induce her to marry into a family that allowed such a horrible phantom to walk up and down the terrace at twilight. Poor Jack was afterwards shot in a duel by Lord Canterville on Wandsworth Common, and Lady Barbara died of a broken heart at Tunbridge Wells before the year was out, so, in every way, it had been a great success. It was, however, an extremely difficult "make-up," if I may use such a theatrical expression in connection with one of the greatest mysteries of the supernatural, or, to employ a more scientific term, the higher-natural world, and it took him fully three hours to make his preparations. At last everything was ready, and he was very pleased with his appearance. The big leather riding-boots that went with the dress were just a little too large for him, and he could only find one of the two horse-pistols, but, on the whole, he was quite satisfied, and at a quarter-past one he glided out of the wainscoting and crept down the corridor. On reaching the room occupied by the twins, which I should mention was called the Blue Bed Chamber, on account of the color of its hangings, he found the door just ajar. Wishing to make an effective entrance, he flung it wide open, when a heavy jug of water fell right down on him, wetting him to the skin, and just missing his left shoulder by a couple of inches. At the same moment he heard stifled shrieks of laughter proceeding from the four-post bed. The shock to his nervous system was so great that he fled back to his room as hard as he could go, and the next day he was laid up with a severe cold. The only thing that at all consoled him in the whole affair was the fact that he had not brought his head with him, for, had he done so, the consequences might have been very serious.

He now gave up all hope of ever frightening this rude American family, and contented himself, as a rule, with creeping about the passages in list slippers, with a thick red muffler round his throat for fear of drafts, and a small arquebuse, in case he should be attacked by the twins. The final blow he received occurred on the 19th of September. He had gone down-stairs to the great entrance-hall, feeling sure that there, at any rate, he would be quite unmolested, and was amusing himself by making satirical remarks on the large Saroni photographs of the United States Minister and his wife, which had now taken the place of the Canterville family pictures. He was simply but neatly clad in a long shroud, spotted with churchyard mould, had tied up his jaw with a strip of yellow linen, and carried a small lantern and a sexton's spade. In fact, he was dressed for the character of "Jonas the Graveless, or the Corpse-Snatcher of Chertsey Barn," one of his most remarkable impersonations, and one which the Cantervilles had every reason to remember, as it was the real origin of their quarrel with their neighbor, Lord Rufford. It was about a quarter-past two o'clock in the morning, and, as far as he could ascertain, no one was stirring. As he was strolling towards the library, however, to see if there were any traces left of the blood-stain, suddenly there leaped out on him from a dark corner two figures, who waved their arms wildly above their heads, and shrieked out "BOO!" in his ear.

Seized with a panic, which, under the circumstances, was only natural, he rushed for the staircase, but found Washington Otis waiting for him there with the big garden-syringe, and being thus hemmed in by his enemies on every side, and driven almost to bay, he vanished into the great iron stove, which, fortunately for him, was not lit, and had to make his way home through the flues and chimneys, arriving at his own room in a terrible state of dirt, disorder, and despair.

After this he was not seen again on any nocturnal expedition.

The twins lay in wait for him on several occasions, and strewed the passages with nutshells every night to the great annoyance of their parents and the servants, but it was of no avail. It was quite evident that his feelings were so wounded that he would not appear. Mr. Otis consequently resumed his great work on the history of the Democratic Party, on which he had been engaged for some years; Mrs. Otis organized a wonderful clam-bake, which amazed the whole county; the boys took to lacrosse, euchre, poker, and other American national games, and Virginia rode about the lanes on her pony, accompanied by the young Duke of Cheshire, who had come to spend the last week of his holidays at Canterville Chase. It was generally assumed that the ghost had gone away, and, in fact, Mr. Otis wrote a letter to that effect to Lord Canterville, who, in reply, expressed his great pleasure at the news, and sent his best congratulations to the Minister's worthy wife.

The Otises, however, were deceived, for the ghost was still in the house, and though now almost an invalid, was by no means ready to let matters rest, particularly as he heard that among the guests was the young Duke of Cheshire, whose grand-uncle, Lord Francis Stilton, had once bet a hundred guineas with Colonel Carbury that he would play dice with the Canterville ghost, and was found the next morning lying on the floor of the card-room in such a helpless paralytic state that, though he lived on to a great age, he was never able to say anything again but "Double Sixes." The story was well known at the time, though, of course, out of respect to the feelings of the two noble families, every attempt was made to hush it up, and a full account of all the circumstances connected with it will be found in the third volume of Lord Tattle's *Recollections of the Prince Regent and his Friends*. The ghost, then, was naturally very anxious to show that he had not lost his influence over the

Stiltons, with whom, indeed, he was distantly connected, his own first cousin having been married *en secondes noces* to the Sieur de Bulkeley, from whom, as every one knows, the Dukes of Cheshire are lineally descended. Accordingly, he made arrangements for appearing to Virginia's little lover in his celebrated impersonation of "The Vampire Monk, or the Bloodless Benedictine," a performance so horrible that when old Lady Startup saw it, which she did on one fatal New Year's Eve, in the year 1764, she went off into the most piercing shrieks, which culminated in violent apoplexy, and died in three days, after disinheriting the Cantervilles, who were her nearest relations, and leaving all her money to her London apothecary. At the last moment, however, his terror of the twins prevented his leaving his room, and the little Duke slept in peace under the great feathered canopy in the Royal Bedchamber, and dreamed of Virginia.

V

A FEW days after this, Virginia and her curly-haired cavalier went out riding on Brockley meadows, where she tore her habit so badly in getting through a hedge that, on their return home, she made up her mind to go up by the back staircase so as not to be seen. As she was running past the Tapestry Chamber, the door of which happened to be open, she fancied she saw someone inside, and thinking it was her mother's maid, who sometimes used to bring her work there, looked in to ask her to mend her habit. To her immense surprise, however, it was the Canterville Ghost himself! He was sitting by the window, watching the ruined gold of the yellowing trees fly through the air, and the red leaves dancing madly down the long avenue. His head was leaning on his hand, and his whole attitude was one of extreme depression. Indeed, so forlorn, and so much out of repair did he look, that little Virginia, whose first idea had been to run away and lock herself in her room, was filled with pity, and determined to try and comfort him. So light was her footfall, and so deep his melancholy, that he was not aware of her presence till she spoke to him.

"I am so sorry for you," she said, "but my brothers are going back to Eton to-morrow, and then, if you behave yourself, no one will annoy you."

"It is absurd asking me to behave myself," he answered, looking round in astonishment at the pretty little girl who had ventured to address him, "quite absurd. I must rattle my chains, and groan through keyholes, and walk about at night, if that is what you mean. It is my only reason for existing."

"It is no reason at all for existing, and you know you have been very wicked. Mrs. Umney told us, the first day we arrived here, that you had killed your wife."

"Well, I quite admit it," said the Ghost, petulantly, "but it was a purely family matter, and concerned no one else."

"It is very wrong to kill any one," said Virginia, who at times had a sweet puritan gravity, caught from some old New England ancestor.

"Oh, I hate the cheap severity of abstract ethics! My wife was very plain, never had my ruffs properly starched, and knew nothing about cookery. Why, there was a buck I had shot in Hogley Woods, a magnificent pricket, and do you know how she had it sent to table? However, it is no matter now, for it is all over, and I don't think it was very nice of her brothers to starve me to death, though I did kill her."

"Starve you to death? Oh, Mr. Ghost—I mean Sir Simon, are you hungry? I have a sandwich in my case. Would you like it ?"

"No, thank you, I never eat anything now; but it is very kind of you, all the same, and you are much nicer than the rest of your horrid, rude, vulgar, dishonest family."

"Stop!" cried Virginia, stamping her foot, "it is you who are rude, and horrid, and vulgar, and as for dishonesty, you know you stole the paints out of my box to try and furbish up that ridiculous blood-stain in the library. First you took all my reds, including the vermilion, and I couldn't do any more sunsets, then you took the emerald green and the chrome-yellow, and finally I had nothing left but indigo and Chinese white, and could only do moonlight scenes, which are always depressing to look at, and not at all easy to paint. I never told on you, though I was very much annoyed, and it was most ridiculous, the whole thing; for who ever heard of emerald-green blood ?"

"Well, really," said the Ghost, rather meekly, "what was I to do? It is a very difficult thing to get real blood nowadays, and, as your brother began it all with his Paragon Detergent, I certainly saw no reason why I should not have your paints. As for color, that is always a matter of taste: the Cantervilles have blue blood, for instance, the very bluest in England; but I know you Americans don't care for things of this kind."

"You know nothing about it, and the best thing you can do is to emigrate and improve your mind. My father will be only too happy to give you a free passage, and though there is a heavy duty on spirits of every kind, there will be no difficulty about the Custom House, as the officers are all Democrats. Once in New York, you are sure to be a great success. I know lots of people there who would give a hundred thousand dollars to have a grandfather, and much more than that to have a family ghost."

"I don't think I should like America."

"I suppose because we have no ruins and no curiosities," said Virginia, satirically.

"No ruins! no curiosities!" answered the Ghost; "you have your navy and your manners."

"Good evening; I will go and ask papa to get the twins an extra week's holiday."

"Please don't go, Miss Virginia," he cried; "I am so lonely and so unhappy, and I really don't know what to do. I want to go to sleep and I cannot."

"That's quite absurd! You have merely to go to bed and blow out the candle. It is very difficult sometimes to keep awake, especially at church, but there is no difficulty at all about sleeping. Why, even babies know how to do that, and they are not very clever."

"I have not slept for three hundred years," he said sadly, and Virginia's beautiful blue eyes opened in wonder; "for three hundred years I have not slept, and I am so tired."

Virginia grew quite grave, and her little lips trembled like rose-leaves. She came towards him, and kneeling down at his side, looked up into his old withered face.

"Poor, poor Ghost," she murmured; "have you no place where you can sleep ?"

"Far away beyond the pinewoods," he answered, in a low, dreamy voice, "there is a little garden. There the grass grows long and deep, there are the great white stars of the hemlock flower, there the nightingale sings all night long. All night long he sings, and the cold crystal moon looks down, and the yew-tree spreads out its giant arms over the sleepers."

Virginia's eyes grew dim with tears, and she hid her face in her hands.

"You mean the Garden of Death," she whispered.

"Yes, death. Death must be so beautiful. To lie in the soft brown earth, with the grasses waving above one's head, and listen to silence. To have no yesterday, and no to-morrow. To forget time, to forget life, to be at peace. You can help me. You can open for me the portals of death's house, for love is always with you, and love is stronger than death is."

Virginia trembled, a cold shudder ran through her, and for a few moments there was silence. She felt as if she was in a terrible dream.

Then the Ghost spoke again, and his voice sounded like the sighing of the wind.

"Have you ever read the old prophecy on the library window?"

"Oh, often," cried the little girl, looking up; "I know it quite well. It is painted in curious black letters, and is difficult to read. There are only six lines:

> When a golden girl can win
> Prayer from out the lips of sin,
> When the barren almond bears,
> and a little child gives away its tears,
> Then shall all the house be still
> And peace come to Canterville.

But I don't know what they mean."

"They mean," he said, sadly, "that you must weep with me for my sins, because I have no tears, and pray with me for my soul, because I have no faith, and then, if you have always been sweet, and good, and gentle, the Angel of Death will have mercy on me. You will see fearful shapes in darkness, and wicked voices will whisper in your ear, but they will not harm you, for against the purity of a little child the powers of Hell cannot prevail."

Virginia made no answer, and the ghost wrung his hands in wild despair as he looked down at her bowed golden head. Suddenly she stood up, very pale, and with a strange light in her eyes. "I am not afraid," she said firmly, "and I will ask the Angel to have mercy on you."

He rose from his seat with a faint cry of joy, and taking her hand bent over it with old-fashioned grace and kissed it. His fingers were as cold as ice, and his lips burned like fire, but Virginia did not falter, as he led her across the dusky room. On the faded green tapestry were embroidered little huntsmen. They blew their tasselled horns and with their tiny hands waved to her to go back. "Go back! little Virginia," they cried, "go back!" but the Ghost clutched her hand more tightly, and she shut her eyes against them. Horrible animals with lizard tails and goggle eyes blinked at her from the carven chimneypiece, and murmured, "Beware! little Virginia, beware! we may never see you again," but the Ghost glided on more swiftly, and Virginia did not listen. When they reached the end of the room he stopped, and muttered some words she could not understand. She opened her eyes, and saw the wall slowly fading away like a mist, and a great black cavern in front of her. A bitter cold wind swept round them, and she felt something pulling at her dress. "Quick, quick," cried the Ghost, "or it will be too late," and in a moment the wainscoting had closed behind them, and the Tapestry Chamber was empty.

VI

ABOUT ten minutes later, the bell rang for tea, and, as Virginia did not come down, Mrs. Otis sent up one of the footmen to tell her. After a little time he returned and said that he could not find Miss Virginia anywhere. As she was in the habit of going out to the garden every evening to get flowers for the dinner-table, Mrs. Otis was not at all alarmed at first, but when six o'clock struck, and Virginia did not appear, she became really agitated, and sent the boys out to look for her, while she herself and Mr. Otis searched every room in the house. At half-past six the boys came back and said that they could find no trace of their sister anywhere. They were all now in the greatest state of excitement, and did not know what to do, when Mr. Otis suddenly remembered that, some few days before, he had given a band of gypsies permission to camp in the park. He accordingly at once set off for Blackfell Hollow, where he knew they were, accompanied by his eldest son and two of the farm-servants. The little Duke of Cheshire, who was perfectly frantic with anxiety, begged hard to be allowed to go too, but Mr. Otis would not allow him, as he was afraid there might be a scuffle. On arriving at the spot, however, he found that the gypsies had gone, and it was evident that their departure had been rather sudden, as the fire was still burning, and some plates were lying on the grass. Having sent off Washington and the two men to scour the district, he ran home, and despatched telegrams to all the police inspectors in the county, telling them to look out for a little girl who had been kidnapped by tramps or gypsies. He then ordered his horse to be brought round, and, after insisting on his wife and the three boys sitting down to dinner, rode off down the Ascot road with a groom. He had hardly, however, gone a couple of miles, when he heard somebody galloping after him, and, looking round, saw the little Duke coming up on his pony, with his face very flushed, and no hat. "I'm awfully sorry, Mr. Otis," gasped out the boy, "but I can't eat any dinner as long as Virginia is lost. Please, don't be angry with me; if you had let us be engaged last year, there would never have been all this trouble. You won't send me back, will you? I can't go! I won't go!"

The Minister could not help smiling at the handsome young scapegrace, and was a good deal touched at his devotion to Virginia, so leaning down from his horse, he patted him kindly on the shoulders, and said, "Well, Cecil, if you won't go back, I suppose you must come with me, but I must get you a hat at

Ascot."

"Oh, bother my hat! I want Virginia!" cried the little Duke, laughing, and they galloped on to the railway station. There Mr. Otis inquired of the station-master if any one answering to the description of Virginia had been seen on the platform, but could get no news of her. The station-master, however, wired up and down the line, and assured him that a strict watch would be kept for her, and, after having bought a hat for the little Duke from a linen-draper, who was just putting up his shutters, Mr. Otis rode off to Bexley, a village about four miles away, which he was told was a well-known haunt of the gypsies, as there was a large common next to it. Here they roused up the rural policeman, but could get no information from him, and, after riding all over the common, they turned their horses' heads homewards, and reached the Chase about eleven o'clock, dead-tired and almost heart-broken. They found Washington and the twins waiting for them at the gate-house with lanterns, as the avenue was very dark. Not the slightest trace of Virginia had been discovered. The gypsies had been caught on Brockley meadows, but she was not with them, and they had explained their sudden departure by saying that they had mistaken the date of Chorton Fair, and had gone off in a hurry for fear they should be late. Indeed, they had been quite distressed at hearing of Virginia's disappearance, as they were very grateful to Mr. Otis for having allowed them to camp in his park, and four of their number had stayed behind to help in the search. The carp-pond had been dragged, and the whole case thoroughly gone over, but without any result. It was evident that, for that night at any rate, Virginia was lost to them; and it was in a state of the deepest depression that Mr. Otis and the boys walked up to the house, the groom following behind with the two horses and the pony. In the hall they found a group of frightened servants, and lying on a sofa in the library was poor Mrs. Otis, almost out of her mind with terror and anxiety, and having her forehead bathed with eau de cologne by the old housekeeper. Mr. Otis at once insisted on her having something to eat, and ordered up supper for the whole party. It was a melancholy meal, as hardly any one spoke, and even the twins were awe-struck and subdued, as they were very fond of their sister. When they had finished, Mr. Otis, in spite of the entreaties of the little Duke, ordered them all to bed, saying that nothing more could be done that night, and that he would telegraph in the morning to Scotland Yard for some detectives to be sent down immediately. Just as they were passing out of the dining-room, midnight began to boom from the clock tower, and when the last stroke sounded they heard a crash and a sudden shrill cry; a dreadful peal of thunder shook the house, a strain of unearthly music floated through the air, a panel at the top of the staircase flew back with a loud noise, and out on the landing, looking very pale and white, with a little casket in her hand, stepped Virginia. In a moment they had all rushed up to her. Mrs. Otis clasped her passionately in her arms, the Duke smothered her with violent kisses, and the twins executed a wild war-dance round the group.

"Good heavens! child, where have you been?" said Mr. Otis, rather angrily, thinking that she had been playing some foolish trick on them. "Cecil and I have been riding all over the country looking for you, and your mother has been frightened to death. You must never play these practical jokes any more."

"Except on the Ghost! except on the Ghost!" shrieked the twins, as they capered about.

"My own darling, thank God you are found; you must never leave my side again," murmured Mrs. Otis, as she kissed the trembling child, and smoothed the tangled gold of her hair.

"Papa," said Virginia, quietly, "I have been with the Ghost.

He is dead, and you must come and see him. He had been very wicked, but he was really sorry for all that he had done, and he gave me this box of beautiful jewels before he died."

The whole family gazed at her in mute amazement, but she was quite grave and serious; and, turning round, she led them through the opening in the wainscoting down a narrow secret corridor, Washington following with a lighted candle, which he had caught up from the table. Finally, they came to a great oak door, studded with rusty nails. When Virginia touched it, it swung back on its heavy hinges, and they found themselves in a little low room, with a vaulted ceiling, and one tiny grated window. Imbedded in the wall was a huge iron ring, and chained to it was a gaunt skeleton, that was stretched out at full length on the stone floor, and seemed to be trying to grasp with its long fleshless fingers an old-fashioned trencher and ewer, that were placed just out of its reach. The jug had evidently been once filled with water, as it was covered inside with green mould. There was nothing on the trencher but a pile of dust. Virginia knelt down beside the skeleton, and, folding her little hands together, began to pray silently, while the rest of the party looked on in wonder at the terrible tragedy whose secret was now disclosed to them.

"Hallo!" suddenly exclaimed one of the twins, who had been looking out of the window to try and discover in what wing of the house the room was situated. "Hallo! the old withered almond-tree has blossomed. I can see the flowers quite plainly in the moonlight."

"God has forgiven him," said Virginia, gravely, as she rose to her feet, and a beautiful light seemed to illumine her face.

"What an angel you are!" cried the young Duke, and he put his arm round her neck, and kissed her.

VII

FOUR days after these curious incidents, a funeral started from Canterville Chase at about eleven o'clock at night. The hearse was drawn by eight black horses, each of which carried on its head a great tuft of nodding ostrich-plumes, and the leaden coffin was covered by a rich purple pall, on which was embroidered in gold the Canterville coat-of-arms. By the side of the hearse and the coaches walked the servants with lighted torches, and the whole procession was wonderfully impressive. Lord Canterville was the chief mourner, having come up specially from Wales to attend the funeral, and sat in the first carriage along with little Virginia. Then came the United States Minister and his wife, then Washington and the three boys, and in the last carriage was Mrs. Umney. It was generally felt that, as she had been frightened by the ghost for more than fifty years of her life, she had a right to see the last of him. A deep grave had been dug in the corner of the churchyard, just under the old yew-tree, and the service was read in the most impressive manner by the Rev. Augustus Dampier. When the ceremony was over, the servants, according to an old custom observed in the Canterville family, extinguished their torches, and, as the coffin was being lowered into the grave, Virginia stepped forward, and laid on it a large cross made of white and pink almond-blossoms. As she did so, the moon came out from behind a cloud, and flooded with its silent silver the little churchyard, and from a distant copse a nightingale began to sing. She thought of the ghost's description of the Garden of Death, her eyes became dim with tears, and she hardly spoke a word during the drive home.

The next morning, before Lord Canterville went up to town, Mr. Otis had an interview with him on the subject of the jewels the ghost had given to Virginia. They were perfectly magnificent, especially a certain ruby necklace with old Venetian setting, which was really a superb specimen of sixteenth-century work, and their value was so great that Mr. Otis felt considerable scruples about allowing his daughter to accept them.

"My lord," he said, "I know that in this country mortmain is held to apply to trinkets as well as to land, and it is quite clear to me that these jewels are, or should be, heirlooms in your family. I must beg you, accordingly, to take them to London with you, and to regard them simply as a portion of your property which has been restored to you under certain strange conditions. As for my daughter, she is merely a child, and has as yet, I am glad to say, but little interest in such appurtenances of idle luxury, I am also informed by Mrs. Otis, who, I may say, is no mean authority upon Art,—having had the privilege of spending several winters in Boston when she was a girl,—that these gems are of great monetary worth, and if offered for sale would fetch a tall price. Under these circumstances, Lord Canterville, I feel sure that you will recognize how impossible it would be for me to allow them to remain in the possession of any member of my family; and, indeed, all such vain gauds and toys, however suitable or necessary to the dignity of the British aristocracy, would be completely out of place among those who have been brought up on the severe, and I believe immortal, principles of Republican simplicity. Perhaps I should mention that Virginia is very anxious that you should allow her to retain the box, as a memento of your unfortunate but misguided ancestor. As it is extremely old, and consequently a good deal out of repair, you may perhaps think fit to comply with her request. For my own part, I confess I am a good deal surprised to find a child of mine expressing sympathy with medievalism in any form, and can only account for it by the fact that Virginia was born in one of your London suburbs shortly after Mrs. Otis had returned from a trip to Athens."

Lord Canterville listened very gravely to the worthy Minister's speech, pulling his grey moustache now and then to hide an involuntary smile, and when Mr. Otis had ended, he shook him cordially by the hand, and said: "My dear sir, your charming little daughter rendered my unlucky ancestor, Sir Simon, a very important service, and I and my family are much indebted to her for her marvellous courage and pluck. The jewels are clearly hers, and, egad, I believe that if I were heartless enough to take them from her, the wicked old fellow would be out of his grave in a fortnight, leading me the devil of a life. As for their being heirlooms, nothing is an heirloom that is not so mentioned in a will or legal document, and the existence of these jewels has been quite unknown. I assure you I have no more claim on them than your butler, and when Miss Virginia grows up, I dare say she will be pleased to have pretty things to wear. Besides, you forget, Mr. Otis, that you took the furniture and the ghost at a valuation, and anything that belonged to the ghost passed at once into your possession, as, whatever activity Sir Simon may have shown in the corridor at night, in point of law he was really dead, and you acquired his property by purchase."

Mr. Otis was a good deal distressed at Lord Canterville's refusal, and begged him to reconsider his decision, but the good-natured peer was quite firm, and finally induced the Minister to allow his daughter to retain the present the ghost had given her, and when, in the spring of 1890, the young Duchess of Cheshire was presented at the Queen's first drawing-room on the occasion of her marriage, her jewels were the universal theme of admiration. For Virginia received the coronet, which is the reward of all good little American girls, and was married to her boy-lover as soon as he came of age. They were both so charming, and they loved each other so much, that everyone was delighted at the match, except the old Marchioness of Dumbleton, who had tried to catch the Duke for one of her seven unmarried daughters, and had given no less than three expensive dinner-parties for that purpose, and, strange to say, Mr. Otis himself. Mr. Otis was extremely fond of the young Duke personally, but, theoretically, he objected to titles, and, to use his own words, "was not without apprehension lest, amid the enervating influences of a pleasure-loving aristocracy, the true principles of Republican simplicity should be forgotten." His objections, however, were completely overruled, and I believe that when he walked up the aisle of St. George's, Hanover Square, with his daughter leaning on his arm, there was not a prouder man in the whole length and breadth of England.

The Duke and Duchess, after the honeymoon was over, went down to Canterville Chase, and on the day after their arrival they walked over in the afternoon to the lonely churchyard by the pine woods. There had been a great deal of difficulty at first about the inscription on Sir Simon's tombstone, but finally it had been decided to engrave on it simply the initials of the old gentleman's name, and the verse from the library window. The Duchess had brought with her some lovely roses, which she strewed upon the grave, and after they had stood by it for some time they strolled into the ruined chancel of the old abbey. There the Duchess sat down on a fallen pillar while her husband lay at her feet smoking a cigarette and looking up at her beautiful eyes. Suddenly he threw his cigarette away, took hold of her hand, and said to her, "Virginia, a wife should have no secrets from her husband."

"Dear Cecil! I have no secrets from you."

"Yes, you have," he answered, smiling, "you have never told me what happened to you when you were locked up with the ghost."

"I have never told anyone, Cecil," said Virginia, gravely.

"I know that, but you might tell me."

"Please don't ask me, Cecil, I cannot tell you. Poor Sir Simon! I owe him a great deal. Yes, don't laugh, Cecil, I really do. He made me see what Life is, and what Death signifies, and why Love is stronger than both."

The Duke rose and kissed his wife lovingly.

"You can have your secret as long as I have your heart," he murmured.

"You have always had that, Cecil."

"And you will tell our children some day, won't you ?"

Virginia blushed.

Index